HOLDING THE DREAM

TETON MOUNTAIN SERIES
BOOK 3

KELLIE COATES GILBERT

To Jeramie Ausmus.
Sometimes the sweetest gifts come in surprising packages.

PRAISE FOR KELLIE COATES GILBERT'S NOVELS

"If you're looking for a new author to read, you can't go wrong with Kellie Coates Gilbert."
~**Lisa Wingate**, NY Times bestselling author of *Before We Were Yours*

"Well-drawn, sympathetic characters and graceful language"
~**Library Journal**

"Deft, crisp storytelling"
~**RT Book Reviews**

"I devoured the book in one sitting."
~**Chick Lit Central**

"Gilbert's heartfelt fiction is always a pleasure to read."
~**Buzzing About Books**

"Kellie Coates Gilbert delivers emotionally gripping plots and authentic characters."

~Life Is Story

"I laughed, I cried, I wanted to throw my book against the wall, but I couldn't quit reading."
~Amazon reader

"I have read other books I had a hard time putting down, but this story totally captivated me."
~Goodreads reader

"I became somewhat depressed when the story actually ended. I wanted more."
~Barnes and Noble reader

ALSO BY KELLIE COATES GILBERT

Dear Readers,

Thank you for reading this story. If you'd like to read more of my books, please check out these series.

To purchase at special discounts: www.kelliecoatesgilbertbooks.com

TETON MOUNTAIN SERIES

Where We Belong – Book 1

Echoes of the Heart – Book 2

Holding the Dream – Book 3

As the Sun Rises – Book 4

MAUI ISLAND SERIES

Under the Maui Sky – Book 1

Silver Island Moon – Book 2

Tides of Paradise – Book 3

The Last Aloha – Book 4

Ohana Sunrise – Book 5

Sweet Plumeria Dawn – Book 6

Songs of the Rainbow – Book 7

Hibiscus Christmas – Book 8

PACIFIC BAY SERIES

Chances Are – Book 1

Remember Us – Book 2

Chasing Wind – Book 3

Between Rains – Book 4

SUN VALLEY SERIES

Sisters – Book 1

Heartbeats – Book 2

Changes – Book 3

Promises – Book 4

TEXAS GOLD COLLECTION

A Woman of Fortune – Book 1

Where Rivers Part – Book 2

A Reason to Stay – Book 3

What Matters Most – Book 4

STAND ALONE NOVELS:

Mother of Pearl

AVAILABLE AT ALL MAJOR RETAILERS

FOR EXCLUSIVE DISCOUNTS:

www.kelliecoatesgilbertbooks.com

HOLDING THE DREAM

TETON MOUNTAIN SERIES, BOOK 3

Kellie Coates Gilbert

1

"Mom! Hey, wake up!"

Lila's consciousness fluttered back to the surface, her cheek lifting from the cool press of the kitchen table. "Hmm?" Her voice was groggy, fingers sweeping tiredness from her eyes as she tried to focus.

Camille stood resolute with her hands on her hips. "We need to hurry if we're going to be on time for Reva's ceremony. You promised an early appearance. What kind of a best friend are you if you miss helping her put on her wedding dress?" Her daughter turned towards the kitchen counter, decisive. "Let me handle the coffee. You head for a shower."

With a weary nod, Lila closed her textbook and powered down her laptop. It had become a familiar scene—falling asleep amidst her studies, a reflection of her stretched-thin life balancing single motherhood, a full-time job, and her ambitious pursuit of a degree in veterinary medicine through the University of Colorado's online program. With finals looming, she was on the cusp of finally getting her degree specializing in large animal and equine care, despite knowing it wouldn't necessarily mean a higher income...not if she remained living in Thunder Mountain.

Her footsteps were heavy as she made her way to her bedroom, proof of the exhaustion that clung to her like a second skin. Despite everything, Lila fought to remember her value, a battle made all the harder by the overshadowing presence of her employer, Doc Tillman Strode, and the dated, oppressive atmosphere of his veterinary practice.

She pulled off yesterday's shirt and tossed it onto the growing laundry pile before heading for the bathroom.

Lila stepped into the shower and activated the flow, stifling a gasp as the initial cold cascade touched her skin. Moments later, the stream warmed, and Lila closed her eyes, relishing the sensation of warmth soothing her shoulders.

Time was a precious commodity and seemed to pass more quickly with every year.

Her daughter was now in her senior year in high school. In the spring, she'd be graduating and had her heart set on attending school in Denver. Not any school, but an expensive private college. Even with the financial assistance they were lining up, the cost of attending Colorado College was choking.

Despite the financial strain, Lila couldn't help but feel proud.

Seizing the shampoo bottle, she generously applied it to her hair, working it into a rich lather. As the foam enveloped her scalp, her mind wandered, contemplating the changes that inevitably lay ahead.

Soon Camille would move out and start her own life.

Her daughter aspired to a career in film and media studies, a path bolstered by Nick Thatcher's endorsement and a summer job on his film crew in Jackson. Nick, a veteran of the Los Angeles film scene, had seen potential in Camille, steering her towards the stability of production work over the fleeting allure of acting fame—her original, and ill-sighted, career choice.

Camille had eventually set her sights on becoming an executive producer, a decision that made Lila smile amidst the steam of her shower. In her determination, Camille mirrored her father, Aaron Bellamy—a man never short on confidence.

She shut the water off and immediately heard Camille's voice again. "I've left your coffee by the sink and laid out your dress on the bed. I'll be downstairs packing up the car."

Stepping out of the shower, Lila marveled at the swift role reversal between them. It seemed only yesterday she was coaxing a younger Camille out of bed for school. Now, her daughter was the one ensuring they stayed on track, a poignant reminder of the swift passage of time and the growth her daughter had undergone.

An hour later, as Lila and Camille arrived at Moose Chapel, the parking lot was already filling. They spotted Charlie Grace's pickup and Capri's jeep among the vehicles, with Reva's black Escalade standing out across the way.

"Ready, Mom?" Camille inquired, turning to Lila as the car came to a halt.

A moment of hesitation. "Head inside, I'll follow shortly," Lila responded, her voice betraying a hint of unease.

Camille's expression clouded with puzzled concern. "What's up? Are you sure?"

Lila offered a reassuring nod. "Yes, just need a moment. I'll be right there."

With a lingering look of bewilderment, Camille exited the car and made her way into the chapel.

Alone now, Lila took a deep breath, allowing herself a moment to gather her thoughts.

Grief was sneaky. The emotions could sneak up on you out of nowhere...even all these years later.

Lila glanced around at the familiar scene before her. The rustic log Moose Chapel sat on a rise just within the southern entrance of Grand Teton National Park. A large window behind its altar framed the magnificent beauty of the Teton Mountain Range. It had become a favorite spot for photographers, sightseers, and weddings—and was the place she and everyone in Thunder Mountain gathered on Sunday for worship.

Now, on the morning of Reva's big day, Lila found herself inevitably drawn back to the memory of her own wedding at Moose Chapel.

It was a Saturday, and she was barely twenty years old. She wore a simple V-neck chiffon dress that gracefully swept the floor and cleverly concealed the white cowboy boots she had chosen for the occasion, a whimsical yet heartfelt nod to the matching pair Aaron wore as he awaited her at the altar with the view of the majestic Teton Mountains in the background. His hands were neatly clasped, his posture a blend of anticipation and reverence for the moment unfolding before him. And there, playing upon his lips, was the familiar, endearing grin that she had come to adore.

Lila swallowed the lump in her throat. They thought they had their entire lives ahead to live out their dreams.

And when they found out about the pregnancy, their joy was unmatched. They were creating a life together, a testament to the love they shared.

However, destiny had a different path laid out. Aaron's tragic death in a helicopter crash in Fallujah left Lila shattered, her dreams and future hopes with Aaron disintegrating in an instant.

Losing someone you loved that much changed your entire life...especially when your spouse was also your best friend. In those early days, she'd felt completely lost and paralyzed, even when making minor decisions. The bed felt huge...and she hugged his pillow for comfort. Comfort that never came. She didn't feel she could possibly survive. But deep down she knew she had no choice.

And she had survived. She'd gone on without Aaron. She'd raised their baby daughter, got a job, and paid the bills. She'd planned birthday parties and played Santa. Nights melded into an ever-changing mosaic of frightened vigil by a fevered child's bedside followed by anxiously waiting for the tardy return of a fledgling teen driver stretching her wings. Somehow, by the grace of God, she did what had to be done.

Still, the void never went away—as she was poignantly reminded today.

Another car pulled in drawing Lila's attention back to the present. She recognized Earl Dunlop, a large, gruff man—a confirmed bachelor who ran the county snow removal fleet in the winter and served as the chapel's custodian. After checking her makeup in the rearview mirror, she climbed out of the car, smoothed her dress, and headed inside.

"Where have you been?" Capri demanded the minute Lila opened the door to the dressing area. Her friend pointed to her watch. "I'm even here on time. What's up with you being late?"

"Mom was up all night studying," Camille announced in her defense.

Charlie Grace peeked from behind her camera mounted on a tripod. "It doesn't matter. You're here now."

The morning sunlight filtered through the stained-glass windows of Moose Chapel, casting a mosaic of colors across the wooden floor. The air was filled with a palpable sense of giddy excitement and a hint of floral perfume.

Reva stood in the center of the tight, yet cozy, bridal room adorned with vintage décor. She turned, her face filled with emotion. "This is a dream...a day I never expected would materialize," she admitted. Her eyes grew moist.

"Don't start that," Lila told her, grabbing a tissue from the box on the nearby table. She dabbed at her friend's eyes. "You'll ruin your makeup."

Charlie Grace, Lila, and Capri fluttered around her like a trio of joyful butterflies, each one meticulously attending to different aspects of Reva's preparation. Charlie Grace tested the aperture on the camera and then moved to adjust the intricate folds of lace on Reva's veil before clicking off a few shots.

Lila double-checked the emergency kit—Band-Aids, sewing materials, and the like—just in case someone stepped on the hem of Reva's dress and caused a rip. Capri, with her infectious laughter, set the mood by turning on a playlist she'd stored on her phone—some of their favorite songs from high school. As Cyndi Lauper's "Girls Just Want to Have Fun" played, she grabbed Camille's hands and broke into a dance move that made everyone giggle.

In the corner of the room, Lucan, Reva's newly adopted toddler son, was a spectacle of cuteness in his miniature suit. He discovered his reflection in the floor-length mirror and was conversing in a babble only he understood. Every so often, he'd utter a phrase that resembled something coherent.

Suddenly, he turned and pointed to Reva. "Mommy pretty dress." He pulled on his tie. "Big tie."

The room erupted in laughter, and Reva, looking every bit the radiant bride, scooped Lucan into her arms, peppering his cheeks with kisses. "Yes, my love. Your tie is very big and very handsome, just like you!"

Charlie Grace captured the moment on camera, declaring, "Too precious for words."

As they continued their preparations, the women shared stories and memories, their laughter and chatter creating a symphony of happiness. Charlie Grace handed Reva her white gloves. "Remember when I married Gibbs, and he forgot the ring?"

Lila nodded, the corners of her eyes crinkling with amusement. "I sure do. We had to send your dad racing to Gibbs' place in that old blue truck of his to grab it. The ceremony was delayed by a half hour."

Reva shook her head. "I can't believe he forgot it."

"Too bad he also forgot his vows," Capri muttered under her breath.

Charlie Grace gave her a playful shove. "Maybe so, but it all ended well. He married Lizzy, and they have a new little boy. I have our sweet Jewel and hunky Nick Thatcher." She smiled. "It's all good."

Capri reluctantly nodded. "You got the better end of that stick. Gibbs never deserved you."

Charlie Grace waved off her comment. She handed Reva a small, blue ribbon, a last-minute 'something blue' to weave into her all-white rose bouquet. "For luck, and love...always."

Despite the light mood, a wave of emotion washed over Reva, her eyes glistening with tears of joy. Her friends quickly enveloped her in a group hug, their bond unspoken but as tangible as the wedding gown she wore.

Lila looked around at the group of friends, her voice soft but firm. "We've been through so much together. High school, heartbreaks, late-night gab sessions, and now this. Our friendship is such a gift."

Reva nodded and wiped at her cheeks. "The very best kind of gift."

Lucan broke from Reva's hold and toddled over to the door. "Weddy, set, go!"

Laughter filled the room again, and Reva knelt to bring Lucan to eye level. "Yes, my heart. We're ready. Let's go get married to Kellen."

With a final round of touch-ups and lipstick reapplications, the women were ready. They formed a procession, with Lucan leading the way, his steps small but determined.

As the four of them exited the bridal room, the corridor

leading to the tiny chapel was awash with soft light filtering in from the large window behind the altar.

Lila couldn't help but smile.

The day ahead was not just a celebration of Reva's union with Kellen, but a tribute to the journey they had shared—a journey marked with laughter, support, and the unbreakable bond of friendship.

2

"I now pronounce you husband and wife." Pastor Pete gave a triumphant smile. "Kellen, you may now kiss your bride."

Kellen's grin rivaled Pete's as he drew Reva into an embrace and sealed their promises with a kiss.

Little Lucan could be still no longer. He wrangled free of Aunt Mo's arms and scrambled from the front row to join the happy couple. "Me some. Me kiss!"

Laughter rang out as Kellen scooped the little boy into his arms and planted a kiss on one cheek while Reva brushed her lips against his other side. Lucan squealed with delight.

Pastor Pete closed his Bible. With a wide smile, he announced, "We'll see everyone at Thunder Mountain's new Community Center for the reception."

The guests filtered out of the tiny chapel, including Lila and her daughter. "That was beautiful, wasn't it Mom?"

Lila responded with a gentle nod. "Yes, it really was."

Camille swung her purse and smiled. "Especially when Pastor Pete quoted Dory in *Finding Nemo*. 'When I look at you, I can feel it. I look at you, and I'm home.'"

Settling into her car, Lila reflected on her daughter's senti-
mentality and affection for the popular Disney movie. When
she was little, she'd watched the film over and over, worried
that the rambunctious orange fish would never find its way
back. Every time the ending credits would roll, she'd turn and
say, "Again, Mommy. Play it again."

A wave of introspection washed over Lila. She looked over
in the direction of the passenger seat. Despite being single all
these years, she had Camille. Her daughter was her heart's
home.

Minutes later, they pulled into the parking lot of the new
Community Center.

The center was Reva's latest crowning achievement. She
and the rest of the city team had worked diligently for months
on the plans and construction. Even when Reva's office flooded
and had to be rebuilt, she never missed a beat and brought the
project in on time. It was only fitting that the first event to be
held would be Reva's wedding reception.

Inside, Oma Griffith, Betty Dunning, and Dorothy Vaughn
were busy guiding everyone into the multi-purpose hall. The
large space was decorated with pastel balloons and crepe paper
streamers, an instant indication that Reva had turned over the
décor to these ladies known as the Knit Wits—a group of
much-loved town women who fashioned baby booties, lap
blankets, and even dog coats made with multi-colored yarn...all
made with love with sales proceeds donated to a benevolence
fund maintained down at the bank to help neighbors in need.

Tables cloaked in elegant linens graced the southern wall,
each one brimming with an array of potluck dishes, demon-
strating Reva's thoughtful decision to set aside her refined
tastes in favor of fostering a sense of community inclusion on
her special day.

The atmosphere was electric with anticipation, laughter,
and the soft hum of heartfelt conversations as the townsfolk of

Thunder Mountain gathered to celebrate Reva and Kellen's wedding.

Pastor Pete, having led the ceremony earlier, stood by his wife, Annie. "Wasn't it just beautiful, Annie? Reva and Kellen, side by side, it's a match blessed from above," he remarked, his voice filled with emotion.

Annie, her eyes sparkling with happiness, squeezed his hand. "I agree, Pete. Truly a day of love."

Nearby, Fleet Southcott, the town sheriff, shared a hearty laugh with Wooster Cavendish, the town banker, and his wife, Nicola, who had a penchant for gossip. Nicola leaned to Dot Montgomery. "You didn't hear it from me, but Kellen has planned the most extravagant honeymoon. A trip to Maui! Can you imagine? Reva has no idea. She thinks they're going to Sun Valley, Idaho!"

Dot's eyes widened. "You don't say!"

Nicola smugly nodded. "Oh, yes. Apparently, a couple who stayed out at Charlie Grace's Teton Trails Guest Ranch when it first opened will be hosting them at one of the guest houses at their pineapple plantation. And they are going to a big luau that is run by the lady's best friend." Her hand went to her chest. "I would die to take that trip."

Reva, radiant in her wedding dress, was a vision of happiness as she moved through the room, her new husband at her side. Her friends, Charlie Grace, Lila, and Capri formed a tight-knit circle around them, each one taking turns to embrace the couple.

"Oh, Reva, it's been such a magical day," Capri said, her eyes misty.

Charlie Grace chimed in. "We're so happy for you two. Kellen, you better take good care of our girl."

Kellen grinned. "I promise, nothing but the best for her."

Verna Billingsley, Reva's secretary, approached clumsily, nearly tripping over her own feet, a stack of napkins tumbling from her grasp. "Reva, I'm so happy for you," she stammered as she caught herself before falling.

Reva hugged her tightly. "Thank you, Verna. Today wouldn't have been the same without you."

As the afternoon progressed into evening, Kellen took to the center, glass in hand, signaling for quiet. "I want to thank each of you for being here, for supporting us, and for being an integral part of our journey. To my beautiful wife, Reva, you are my everything. Here's to a lifetime of love, laughter, and happiness." Cheers and clinks of glasses filled the room.

The moment everyone had been anticipating arrived as Reva prepared to throw the wedding bouquet. A crowd of hopefuls gathered, giggling and jostling gently. With a graceful arc, the bouquet sailed through the air, landing in the surprised arms of Lila.

Gasps and applause broke out as Lila stood, bouquet in hand, her cheeks flushed with surprise and a hint of embarrassment. Pastor Pete's voice rang out, warm and booming, "Looks like you're next, Lila!"

She responded by quickly handing the bouquet to Capri. "Not me," she corrected. "I hate to disappoint, but marriage is not in my future. I don't have the time," she teased.

As the crowd's chuckles faded into the background, a romantic melody began to play over the speakers, soft and slow, filling the space with an intimate aura. All eyes turned towards the dance floor where Kellen and Reva stood, their hands finding each other's in a practiced motion. There was a collective intake of breath from those gathered as the newlyweds stepped into the spotlight, the world around them fading away. It was their moment, the bride and groom dance, a symbol of their first steps together in this new journey. The onlookers watched, some with teary eyes, as the couple moved in perfect harmony, their love palpable in the air.

When their dance ended, the Eagles—not the famous rock

band, but an ensemble made up of townspeople, including Clancy Rivers and Brewster Findley—were joined on stage by Kellen. With an affectionate wink at his bride, he took his place behind his waiting cello and picked up his bow, positioning it with confidence.

Nick Thatcher approached and offered his hand to Charlie Grace. His wavy dark hair, chiseled jawline, and piercing blue eyes were impossibly charming. When he smiled, his eyes crinkled at the corners. "May I have this dance, Miss Rivers."

Charlie Grace barely contained her delight. "I thought you'd never ask."

Aunt Mo picked up little Lucan, who was so tired he could barely keep his head up. "I think I'll take this little one on home with me if that's all right?"

Reva gave her shoulder a grateful squeeze, then kissed the top of her son's head as it rested against Mo's shoulder.

The night continued with dance, laughter, and an abundance of hugs. Amidst the revelry, Lila and her best friends—Charlie Grace, Reva, and Capri—found a serene spot momentarily isolated from the rest of the guests. There, under the soft glow of string lights, they formed a close circle, hands clasped tightly together, embodying a unity that words could scarcely convey.

Charlie Grace's voice was soft but filled with emotion. "Reva, this goes without saying, but we're so ecstatically happy for you and Kellen."

Lila, her eyes gleaming with tears, added, "Reva, your love story inspires us, reminding us of the beauty God has waiting for each one of us." She grinned as she wiped the moisture from her cheeks. "And by beauty, I mean I'd be happy with a raise in my paycheck."

Capri, always the spirited one, squeezed Reva's hand. "Does Kellen understand that he's getting a package deal? I mean, we're still going to meet on Friday nights, right? We've built a fortress of memories over cocktails." She held up her champagne glass. "Here's to many more!"

Reva, moved by their words, found her voice. "I couldn't have dreamed of this day without you all by my side. My wedding day is as much a celebration of our enduring friendship as it is about my new beginning with Kellen. You are my heart, my soul sisters."

They embraced tightly, a silent promise hanging in the air —a pledge of unwavering support, laughter, and love, no matter the paths they would tread.

Suddenly, a loud voice rang out. "Is there a doctor here? We have a medical emergency!"

They all turned to see a crowd forming across the room.

As they rushed across the room to see, Lila found Doc Tillman on the ground. Her hand flew to her chest. "Oh no!"

"I think he's having a heart attack," shouted Fleet Southcott. He pushed the crowd back. "Give him room and call 911."

3

The nearest hospital was in Jackson, a half-hour drive from Thunder Mountain.

Lila paced the cramped waiting room, her hands wringing a tissue until it frayed at the edges. The low murmur of townsfolk filled the air, all huddled in clumps of party dresses and Sunday bests, faces etched with worry. The sterile gray walls, lined with framed pictures of local landscapes, seemed to close in as the clock ticked unbearably slow.

Tillman Strode was a long-time resident of their community and was much loved.

"Never seen Doc look that pale before, not in all my years," old Mr. Argyle muttered from his corner seat, his voice a gravelly whisper that carried weight in the small space.

Beside him, Carol, the secretary down at the bank, nodded, her eyes rimmed red. "He's done so much for us all. Who's gonna look after our animals if something happens to him?" Her question seemed to hang in the air, adding to the thick tension.

Lila moved closer to the group, trying to draw comfort from their proximity. She hugged Betty Dunning's shoulder, who said, "He was just dancing one minute, and then..." She let her words fade.

Lila understood how she felt. The vivid image of Doc Tillman lying collapsed on the floor was sharply etched in her mind as well.

"He's a tough one," Reva reminded, clutching Kellen's hand tightly. The newlyweds looked ashen; their wedding joy overshadowed by the evening's turn. "Remember when Doc had the flu, and he set Ernie's black Lab's broken leg right there on his kitchen table? He'll pull through."

"Yeah, nothing seems to keep him down," added Capri, trying to muster a smile.

Just then, the door to the back swung open, and a young doctor in scrubs stepped into the waiting room. Every head turned, every conversation paused, and a collective breath seemed to be held.

Lila's heart thudded painfully against her ribs as she stepped forward. "Doctor, how is he? Is Doc Tillman going to be all right?"

The doctor smiled, a warm, reassuring curve of his lips that immediately soothed some of her fears. "He's going to be all right," he announced, and a sigh of relief swept through the room like a gust of wind. "It wasn't a heart attack. We found that he had a severe case of dehydration and low blood sugar, probably didn't eat enough with all the wedding festivities. We've given him fluids, and he's already making jokes about needing to remember to drink more water and less coffee."

Laughter, light and relieved, bubbled up among the group, breaking the former tension.

Lila felt her knees go weak with relief. "Can we go in to see him?"

"In a bit," the doctor replied. "He's asking for some coffee, but we told him maybe stick to water for now. He wants to see everyone, though. Said something about not scaring you all like that ever again."

"Typical Doc," Mr. Jacobs chuckled, shaking his head.

Lila smiled, her heart already warming with the news. Doc Tillman wasn't just her employer; he was a pillar in their small community, a steadfast presence in every animal crisis. Today had scared her more than she wanted to admit, but knowing he would recover was the best news they could have received.

"Thank you, Doctor," she said, her voice thick with emotion. The room buzzed with renewed energy as everyone began to share their own stories of Doc's stubbornness and care, a testament to his indelible mark on their lives.

In that cramped waiting room, under the fluorescent lights, Lila felt the strength of their small community, united in their concern and now their relief. Doc would be okay, and so would they.

As the doctor assured everyone that Doc Tillman's condition was not critical, the cramped waiting room began to empty, with residents of Thunder Mountain filing out into the cool evening air. Lila stepped outside, the hospital doors swinging shut behind her, and found herself enveloped by the lingering twilight.

Reva and Kellen were the first she spotted, standing by Kellen's old pickup truck, still decorated with streamers and tin cans that proclaimed 'Just Married.'

"I suppose we should try to salvage what's left of the reception," Reva said, managing a smile as Lila approached.

Kellen nodded, rubbing the back of his neck. "Yeah, though I reckon the mood might be a bit different now."

Lila chuckled softly. "I think everyone will just be relieved to celebrate something good after tonight's scare. Doc would want us to enjoy the party, especially after giving us such a fright."

Reva sighed, her relief evident. "You're right. Let's head back and make the best of it. Doc's health scare reminded us all how quickly things can change."

Charlie Grace joined them, her car keys jangling in her hand. "I'm ready for a piece of that wedding cake. Nothing like a bit of high-calorie food to lighten the mood."

"And I'll make sure the band stays a while longer," Kellen added, his tone more upbeat.

As they discussed their plans, more townsfolk joined in, sharing rides and arranging to return to the reception venue. Mr. Argyle, leaning on his cane, ambled over to Lila.

"You heading back to the party, Lila?" he asked, his voice low and gravelly.

"I wouldn't miss it," Lila replied, smiling softly. "I need to see everyone smiling and laughing again. Plus, I need to tell Doc all about it tomorrow. He'd hate to miss out on the stories." She paused. "You can ride back with me and Camille if you'd like."

He nodded. "Sure, I'd appreciate that."

The three of them slowly walked to Lila's car, a modest sedan parked under a flickering streetlight. "You know, Lila, that man's been like a father to you," Mr. Argyle remarked as he settled into the passenger seat, referring to Doc.

Lila nodded, starting the engine. "He really has. Tonight was a reminder of how much he means to me...to all of us."

To Lila, Doc was more than just her boss. He was a constant in her life, a gruff mentor under whose shadow she had grown both tough and capable. Even so, their relationship was undoubtedly complex. He could diminish her in one breath and uplift her in another, leaving her to wrestle with feelings of resentment mingled with deep respect.

Losing him would mean not just the loss of her livelihood but the absence of a challenging figure who pushed her limits —both personally and professionally. Despite everything, he was irreplaceable, and the void he would leave behind was unfathomable.

As they drove back to the community center, the streets of Thunder Mountain were quiet, the usual nighttime serenity now tinged with a collective sense of relief and gratitude. The buildings along Main Street seemed to exhale, their aged brick facades relaxing in relief as word spread that Doc was going to be all right.

When they arrived back at the community center, the lights were bright against the dark sky, music filtering out into the parking lot.

"Let's go make some happy memories, for Doc's sake," Lila said, helping Mr. Argyle out of the car. She winked across the top of the car to her daughter, who smiled back.

"That's the spirit," he replied with a grin. They joined the others back into the multi-purpose hall, where the music resumed, a little louder this time, and the laughter began to swell.

Lila linked arms with Camille and, together, they moved through the crowd, each face reflecting relief and joy, a community brought closer by concern and caring. Tonight, they were more than just townsfolk—they were a family, united in their thankfulness that one of their own was safe.

Besides, they had a wedding to celebrate.

4

ila heard a knock and moved for the door. She opened it to find both Capri and Charlie Grace standing there holding covered plates. "You're early," she said as she motioned them inside.

"Oh, hush! We're right on time," Capri said in protest as she headed for Lila's kitchen.

Charlie Grace followed. "As for me, I couldn't get here fast enough. I've had a hellish week. Our reservation system went down out at Teton Trails."

"I heard the entire town's internet was down," Lila reported, taking the plate from Charlie Grace. "You guys want to sit in here at the counter or head for the sofa?"

"Sofa," Capri and Charlie Grace answered in unison.

The group gathered up the plates, glasses, and silverware and headed for the living room. Lila carried a pitcher full of dark pink slush. "I hope you guys like strawberry daiquiris."

Lila's home offered a warm, inviting charm, especially evident in her living room. Despite working with a limited budget, she had transformed the space into a cozy haven. The walls, painted in a soft, sunlit beige, were adorned with a collection of thrifted landscape paintings that captured the rugged beauty of Wyoming's outdoors.

A second-hand, plush sofa draped with a patchwork quilt added a splash of color and a touch of homeyness. A sturdy, well-worn wooden coffee table sat at the center, often graced with a vase of wildflowers Lila plucked from nearby meadows on her morning walks.

The room was lit by carefully chosen lamps found at online discount retailers, their warm glow complementing the natural light that streamed through patterned curtains at the windows.

Each piece in the room, though not costly, was chosen with care and demonstrated Lila's ability to create a beautiful, inviting space on a budget. She had Pinterest to thank for that.

Charlie Grace took the plastic wrap off the plates. "I hadn't heard the internet was down all over town."

"It's still down," Capri told her, shoving a stuffed mushroom into her mouth. "Dang, girl. These are good."

Charlie Grace nodded. "I'd like to take credit, but Aunt Mo deserves the praise. She found the recipe on TikTok."

"TikTok?" Lila scowled. "I heard that phone app spies on you."

"So what?" Capri reached for another mushroom. "I don't have any pictures on my phone they can't see."

"You sure?" Charlie Grace shoulder-bumped her.

"None that I will admit to," Capri shoulder-bumped her back, a little harder.

Lila picked up the pitcher and filled three stemmed glasses. "If the internet remains down, who's going to remedy the situation? Reva's on her honeymoon and won't be back for another week."

Charlie Grace chuckled. "I'm surprised she hasn't learned of it and is trying to make calls from her surfboard."

Lila took her filled glass and snuggled into the cushions of her sofa. "Somehow, I doubt that. She and Kellen have better things to occupy their time with." She grinned.

Charlie Grace took a sip from her glass. "I can't believe they took Lucan with them on the honeymoon. I offered to keep him. So did Aunt Mo."

"I offered as well," Capri said. "The float trips are winding down this late in the season. I easily could have taken some time off."

Lila couldn't help but smile. "I'm not surprised. Do any of us really believe she could be separated from that little guy for two whole weeks?"

Charlie Grace nodded. "Wasn't the adoption ceremony wonderful?"

They all agreed. "I still can't believe Reva is married and is a mommy."

Charlie Grace stirred her drink with her finger. "I hope her new roles don't interfere with our Friday night get-togethers."

"Never!" Capri shook her head in protest. "We all agreed years ago that our nights are sacrosanct." She pointed to her friends. "You've both been married and never let that interrupt our nights."

"Yeah, but this is Reva we're talking about," Charlie Grace reminded.

Lila laughed out loud. "Yes, Reva can be...uh, dedicated to her duties. But I promise you, it won't be too long, and she'll be counting the hours before she can get away for a bit. Being a mother is hard."

Charlie Grace turned to Capri. "Speaking of mothers, how is yours?"

Capri reclined against the sofa cushion, casually propping her boots on the ottoman. Though her posture suggested ease, her eyes betrayed emotions she struggled to conceal.

Capri still lived with her parents. When questioned about

the decision, she shrugged. "It's free." The rest of them knew full well that cash did not weigh in as the deciding factor. Capri owned Grand Teton Whitewater Adventures. She killed it financially, especially during the heavy tourist season. Her chosen profession also left her available in the winters when she alternated filling her time with binging seasons of *Gilmore Girls* on television and snowmobile racing on the local circuit.

Wild adventures aside, Capri dedicated herself to taking care of her mother and stepdad, a man who, thankfully, had replaced his affinity for bourbon with lemonade several years back. Sadly, Dick now fought a cancer diagnosis.

"Mom is doing good. I mean, she has a lot on her plate, with Dick's treatments and all."

"How's Dick doing?" Lila asked.

Capri downed the remainder of her daiquiri in one gulp. She held out her glass to be refilled. "All those years of hard drinking took their toll on his body. And his age isn't a plus. But the treatments seem to be working...for now."

"What drugs are they giving him?" Lila asked.

She went on to explain the treatment options for a horse she'd studied in her coursework, detailing the use of cisplatin or carboplatin, diffusing from beads implanted near the tumor, offering a sustained attack on the cancer cells. She tried to draw parallels to Dick's treatment, suggesting maybe there was something to learn here.

Before she could articulate her thoughts further, Charlie Grace rolled her eyes and dismissed her suggestions "Dick's not a horse."

Lila sighed, frustrated but undeterred. "I'm only saying that I think drugs administered to animals are often overlooked as treatment options. Take ivermectin, for example. I mean, they're learning a lot about that one."

That remark earned a collective groan from her girlfriends. She waved off their dismissal. "Okay, fine. Moving on..."

"Thank you." Capri took a drink of her daiquiri. "If Dick starts craving hay, I'll reach back out to you," she said, half teasing.

Lila cherished the candor of these women who formed the very essence of her heart and soul. They always spoke their minds freely, and even in disagreement, their words and actions were steeped in profound love. She held a deep affection for these girls, more than she could ever fully express.

Charlie Grace picked up the plate filled with toasted baguette slices topped with olive tapenade and offered them to Lila. "And how is Doc Tillman? Has he returned to work?"

"He tried. But his wife was having none of it."

Capri reached for a baguette slice. "Well, he needn't worry. You are more than capable of holding down the fort, so to speak. Besides needing to recuperate, poor Winnie deserves a vacation."

Doc's wife was not one to challenge her husband. Yet, many in town knew she collected travel brochures and dreamed of visiting the Golden Gate Bridge, the Washington Monument in D.C., and strolling the Magic Kingdom in Florida.

Lila had made the mistake of taking up for her once. She'd urged him to take a few weeks away. "I'll keep an eye on things," she told him.

Doc Tillman had scoffed, his skepticism thinly veiled. "Keep an eye on things? Lila, this isn't some weekend hobby or a houseplant you're watering. This is a veterinary practice. It requires more than just good intentions and a warm body." His tone was dismissive, undercutting the confidence Lila had just expressed. "Winnie might need a break, but this clinic needs a professional, a real animal doctor—in case of an emergency." The sharpness in his voice left little room for argument, casting a shadow over the encouragement Lila had offered.

While his remarks stung, she quickly told herself this was his way of maintaining control, of keeping the reins tight even when it might benefit him to let go a little. Lila swallowed the hurt, forcing a placid smile as she responded. "I understand your concerns, Doc, but I assure you I've learned a lot under your guidance. I'm not intending to replace you—I'm just offering to help lighten the load so you and Winnie can take some well-deserved time away."

Despite her diplomatic tone, Lila felt a familiar frustration simmer beneath her calm exterior. It was always the same with Doc Tillman. Her efforts seemed never quite enough to earn his full trust or approval.

Charlie Grace tilted her head and gazed at Lila, likely reading her mind. "Well, Nicola Cavendish was overheard telling someone at the bank that Doc Tillman came in and withdrew some cash. When he was asked about it, he said he was planning a little surprise for Winnie. I don't know if I'm right but sounds like he plans to finally take that poor woman somewhere."

Capri was quick to lean forward and pat Lila's knee. "There you go. Here's your chance to prove yourself to Doc." She and Charlie Grace exchanged glances. "He's got to let go sometime. He can't keep working until he's dead."

As Lila absorbed Capri's words and Charlie Grace's hopeful speculation, a flicker of possibility ignited within her. Could this be her moment to step up and show her worth?

The idea of Doc actually taking time away, leaving her in charge, sent a mix of excitement and anxiety through her veins. She mulled over everything she had learned and all the times she had stood in the background, ready but untested. "He's got to let go sometime," echoed in her mind, mixing with her own desire to grow into more than just an understudy.

As the conversation shifted around her, Lila's thoughts drifted to the stacks of animal patient files she knew by heart, the equipment she could operate with her eyes closed, and the community that depended on their clinic. Yes, she could hope

—more than that, she could prepare. Maybe it was time to step into the light, ready to prove not just to Doc, but to herself, that she was capable of handling more.

This could be her chance to truly make a difference, to stretch her wings and maybe, just maybe, begin to soar.

5

Capri carried the fishing poles and tackle box out to her prized pickup, a bright red Dodge D150 Adventurer 'Lil Red Express Truck she'd brought home from an auction in Denver, all tricked out with oak wood panels, gold pin-striping over the wheel wells, and dual chrome exhaust stacks. The vehicle was her pride and joy.

She secured the poles in the back and headed back for the house. "Okay, Dick," she called out. "We're all loaded up. Let's go."

Seconds later, her stepfather appeared on the arm of her mother. It'd only been months since his diagnosis of liver cancer, yet he was already looking frail and unsteady. Of course, the treatments were aggressive and took their toll. And they didn't even know if the advanced chemotherapeutics would work.

One of the worst parts of the whole thing was that the doctors were almost always guessing. They were smart people, and the guesses were informed by tests and trials and years of experience, but they were guessing nonetheless.

Her mother's face showed signs of worry. "He had a bad night, Capri." There was no missing her concern. "Maybe you should skip going today."

Dick scowled and shook his head. "No. We're going fishing." He retracted his arm from his wife's. "In AA, we learn to live in the present. We can't fix the past or predict the future. There's no promise tomorrow won't be worse. We're going."

Capri's mom's face softened. They exchanged glances, knowing Dick's mind remained firm. There would be no changing it. "Well, then...I hope you both have a wonderful time," she said, lightly patting her husband on the shoulder.

Capri smiled at the sweet gesture.

There was a time when she hated her stepfather. He wasn't the kind of guy who gave you a lot to like.

For years, she'd struggled with her stepdad's alcohol addiction. He was often mean, and his inebriated comments often pierced her armored soul, especially when she attempted to rescue her mother from his verbal assaults.

Thankfully, Dick sobered up years ago after his fourth car accident, where he put a young family in the hospital. The event served as the catalyst for some major changes in his life, not just in his drinking but in how he interacted with his family and friends. Soon, the old Dick gave way to a new version—a man who quietly gained the respect of others.

By the grace of God, she'd grown to forgive and appreciate her stepfather. He was the only dad she'd ever known...and she loved him.

Capri offered Dick her arm. "Well, then ole man...let's go. There's fish waiting to be caught."

They drove out to Jenny Lake and slowly made their way down the trailhead, winding their way through a dense forest of spruce and fir. The air was rich with the scent of pine needles and fresh mountain air. Occasionally, one of them had to duck a low-hanging branch.

The hike was a short thirty minutes. They took it slow, stopping a couple of times to let Dick sit on a nearby rock and rest. As they continued their way along the trail, they passed by a crystal-clear stream that flowed down from the mountains. The water cascading over rocks created a soothing soundtrack.

"You know," Dick said. "Some call the Tetons God's country."

"I wouldn't argue with them," she told him.

Finally, they arrived at their destination—a spot along the lake where the thick blanket of trees gave way to a shoreline of sand and gravel. An area that offered a panoramic view of the water. Long ago, Dick said it was 'their' spot and claimed that it was the best fishing in all of Wyoming.

Turned out he was right. It was a rare occasion that they failed to catch at least a dozen large rainbow trout that day. Of course, Dick had a secret lure...he'd thread the usual earthworm on his hook, but he added a tiny piece of colored marshmallow.

Against the background of the stunning vista, Capri laid the poles against a tree. She slipped the backpack off her shoulders and pulled a fold-up canvas chair from where it was attached with a bungee cord, opened and settled it into the sand, testing to make sure it was sturdy. "There you go, Dick."

He looked at her, grateful, and slipped the backpack off his frail shoulders before sitting. He patted the pack with a veined hand. "Doris said she packed us some bologna sandwiches."

"We won't need any blasted sandwiches, Dick. We're eating fish!"

His face broke into a wide grin. "You betcha. Fish it is!" He unfastened the pack and pulled out a bag of tiny marshmallows. "And maybe a few of these for dessert." He winked.

They settled in, the serene environment enveloping them like a gentle embrace. Capri handed off a pole to Dick and then busied herself baiting her own. She cast her line into the water, the smooth arc punctuated by the gentle plop as the lure hit the lake. Beside her, Dick adjusted in his chair, a contented sigh escaping him as he watched the line disappear into the depths.

"You know, Capri," Dick began, his voice low, almost lost against the whispers of the breeze, "I never thought I'd find peace like this. Not after everything."

Capri glanced over, noting the sun casting a halo around his weary frame. "You've come a long way, Dick. We both have."

"Yeah," he chuckled softly. "Remember how you used to slam your door whenever I tried to talk to you? And now here we are, fishing together. Guess life has a funny way of smoothing out the rough edges."

She smiled, her eyes misty. "I'm glad we got to smooth them out together." Especially now, she thought to herself.

They sat in comfortable silence, the only sound the occasional call of a distant bird and the rhythmic lapping of water against the shore. After a while, Dick spoke again, his voice softer, reflective. "I want you to know something, Capri. I'm sorry for the pain I caused you and your mom. It took me far too long to realize the damage I was doing. But I'm grateful for the second chance. Not everyone gets that."

Capri set her fishing rod down and turned to face him. "I forgave you a long time ago, Dick. You've been more of a father to me than you know. And I love you for it."

Tears welled in Dick's eyes as he reached for her hand, squeezing it gently. "And I love you, kid. More than I ever showed. I'm just...I'm just so proud of the woman you've become."

Capri directed her gaze out at the water for several long seconds. "Are you afraid?"

"Of what's ahead for me? Of dying?"

She nodded almost imperceptibly.

He joined her in gazing out at the beautiful scene before them. "Nah. Ain't nothing to be afraid of. The way I see things,

I'm just moving from one beautiful place to another, one more grand than any earthly landscape. And I have friends there. And my parents. Truth be told, I'm kind of settled about what's to come."

Despite his confident assertion, his eyes filled with unshed tears. "I hate to say goodbye to you and your mother—and some of the old goats I hang with, like Clancy Rivers. But if that Bible your mom keeps on the coffee table is true—and I believe it is—our separation is temporary."

He let out a chuckle. "Besides, I have it on good word that there are a few fishermen up there. I'll spend some time with Peter and the others. We have a lot in common you know. Not only do we like to fish but we've both cut off a few ears in our day before cleaning ourselves up." He winked again—this time with a big smile on his face.

They didn't talk much after that, each lost in their thoughts, soaking in the beauty of the moment and the bittersweet tang of their shared memories.

As the day faded into evening, they managed to catch more than a few fish, just as Dick had promised. Laughing and joking, they cleaned their catch by the lake and cooked up a few using a pan Capri had packed. Before long, the setting sun cast long shadows on the ground.

"It's been a good day, hasn't it?" Dick murmured as they packed up to leave.

"The best," Capri replied, helping him to his feet. "Let's do this again soon."

"Let's," he agreed, though they both understood the unspoken words hanging between them.

They walked back to the truck, arms linked, a steady support for one another. As they drove home, the cabin of the truck filled with the soft glow of the dashboard lights, Capri glanced over at Dick, his face serene, almost radiant.

In that quiet, enduring space between them, filled with love and a deep, unspoken understanding, they reveled in a peace that transcended the need for words. They drove on, tucking the precious memory of their day together in their minds to carry with them forever.

L ila followed Diane Robinson and her daughter from the exam room back into the veterinary clinic's waiting area. "I think Puff Daddy is going to be all right. Just a little feline morning sickness." She winked in Diane's direction.

The little girl buried her face against the furry yellow, and very fat, cat's torso. "Thank you so much! I was so afraid Puff was gonna die."

Her mother smiled. "Honey, I told you—cats rarely die from hurling up their breakfast. Even if three days in a row," her mother told her.

"Your mother's right," Lila added. "Puff Daddy is going to be a mommy."

Despite the irony, the young girl's face brightened with delight. "Which means baby kittens?"

Diane sighed. "Yes, kittens." She leaned toward Lila, hand cupped at her mouth. "My husband is going to have a fit when he finds out."

"We're keeping them," her daughter declared. "All of them."

Diane smiled and patted her young daughter's shoulder.

"We'll see." She turned to Lila. "Tell Doc Tillman that I'll bring him some jars of my pickled rhubarb just as soon as he gets back. Doc loves my pickled rhubarb."

Lila nodded while maintaining a smile on her face. She bid the mother, daughter, and cat goodbye with a wave.

"Too bad canned goods don't pay the bills," she murmured as soon as the door closed behind Diane and her daughter.

Or baked cakes and pies. Or venison jerky.

Lila turned and walked back to the exam room. Doc Tillman could afford more state-of-the-art equipment if he ran a tighter shop. She'd worked for Doc since high school, and as long as she'd known him, he had bartered with anyone who was strapped for cash—which was a lot of the people in Thunder Mountain.

"We have enough to get by," he'd argued when she suggested he might be getting taken advantage of. "The Lord makes sure we have plenty."

While she appreciated his generous spirit, his antiquated vet clinic could use some updating. And she could use a raise more often than every five years.

Lila tore a handful of paper towels from a roll and went to work cleaning the stainless-steel examination table.

While ninety percent of her high school class had fled Thunder Mountain the minute they had their graduation certificate in hand, she had elected to stay. Even after she married. She appreciated the security her hometown provided —especially when Aaron left on his second tour of duty in Afghanistan which left her stateside waiting for him to come home.

She loved Thunder Mountain and the people who had become family. This tiny mountain town was her home. Besides, how could she possibly do life without Charlie Grace, Reva, and Capri—even if leaving might mean a real veterinary career?

Lila noticed the trash can was getting full. She lifted the plastic bag from the container, tied it off, and headed for the back door that led to the dumpster.

Outside, the air was filled with the earthy fall scent of pine and sagebrush that lingered long after the last lupine blooms had faded. The aspens were now showing off their shades of gold and there was a crispness in the air that signaled winter could swoop in and dump snow on the mountain peaks at any time.

Lila took a moment to take it all in, reminding herself once again how lucky she was to live in Thunder Mountain.

Yet, even given all the benefits of residing in a small town, there were also drawbacks.

The produce down at Western Drug and General was rarely fresh, given the trucking times—especially in the winter when the roads made travel treacherous. Thank goodness for summer gardens. Her mind drifted to people who knew how to preserve the fruit and vegetables they grew. And to Diane's canned rhubarb.

Unlike metropolitan areas, Amazon didn't deliver overnight —no matter if you were a Prime member or not. There was no Costco, no Walmart, and only one place to buy clothes.

Apricot Lane, the quaint clothing store nestled in the heart of the tiny mountain town, was a charming relic of simpler times. Owned by Patty Guerard and Barb Miller, it exuded warmth and nostalgia, with its weathered wood exterior and flower-filled window boxes. Inside, the cozy shop was neatly organized, with racks of clothes arranged by season and a rustic counter adorned with a vintage cash register.

Though the selection was limited, focusing on practical mountain wear and a handful of consigned hand-knitted items made by the Knit Wits, Apricot Lane was a beloved stop for both locals and visitors alike. The friendly chatter and laughter of Patty and Barb made every visit feel like catching up with old friends.

The worst drawback of living here in Thunder Mountain was the lack of men. Oh, there were men, all right. But no one Lila might find interesting. Unless she wanted to date Albie Barton or Brewster Findley. Uh...no thanks!

Fortunately, Charlie Grace had better luck. The arrival of Nick Thatcher, a production executive with a television show filming nearby, changed everything for her. His charm and ambition instantly caught her attention. What began as a chance encounter quickly blossomed into something much deeper.

Reva was now on her honeymoon in Maui with Kellen Warner, the charismatic musician slash car mechanic. In a matter of months, she'd fallen in love and became a mother.

Watching Reva and Kellen together, Lila couldn't help but feel hopeful. It was like seeing a fairytale come to life. Lila knew that if anyone deserved this happiness, it was Reva, and she felt privileged to witness her friend find it.

That left her and Capri—still single—still waiting. It was hard not to feel a twinge of envy, but Lila took comfort in knowing that Charlie Grace and Reva finding happiness was proof that love was out there, just waiting for the right moment to find them, too.

Capri's independent streak might relish remaining single, even into her senior years, but Lila hated the thought of Camille leaving the nest and having to grow old alone.

She hoped there would be someone out there for her again someday.

Of course, she had little time to pursue such things. She barely had time to sleep with all that she was currently juggling.

Lila tossed the bag of trash into the dumpster and headed back inside.

"Yoo-hoo. Anyone here?"

Lila rushed to the front to find Nicola Cavendish holding her miniature Yorkshire terrier, a tiny bundle of energy with a glossy long coat and a bright pink bow perched atop its head. "Oh, Lila. I'm so glad you're here," she said, placing her Yorkie into Lila's arms. "It's Sweetpea. She's feeling a bit under the weather," the woman said with a worried expression.

"Oh? How so?" Lila pulled the tiny animal against her chest and petted her.

"Wooster fed her some bacon off his plate this morning. I've told him a thousand times that her little tummy can't take all that fat. Does he listen?" She shook her head vehemently. "No, he does not. My husband is a pushover and lets her have anything she wants, even ice cream. I tell him over and over he must stop indulging our sweet baby." She lovingly clutched Sweetpea's tiny chin. "Isn't that right, baby?"

Lila held back a grin. "Well, let's take a look."

She headed for the exam room in the back with Nicola following at her heels.

Nicola Cavendish had a striking presence, both in appearance and demeanor. Her dark hair was styled into a sleek updo that gave her a touch of old Hollywood glamour. She wore expertly applied makeup, complete with bold lip color and well-defined eyes. Nicola's attire was always polished, favoring tailored designer suits, statement jewelry, and high heels that clicked confidently against the pavement.

She carried herself with an air of confidence that bordered on theatrical, her laugh a sharp, staccato burst that could be heard across the room. Despite her petite stature, she had a commanding presence, often punctuating her sentences with a dramatic gesture or a raised eyebrow. Nicola's demeanor was a mix of charm and mischief, her voice dripping with sarcasm or playful banter as she engaged with the townsfolk, effortlessly weaving through conversations with a wry smile, always leaving others curious about what she would say or do next.

Even more, she prided herself on being in the know about every subject.

"I was on social media yesterday and saw that *Bear Country* will be wrapping up filming their first season soon." Her face went into a pout. "I really liked hanging out on set. Do you think Charlie Grace has heard any inside scoop about a second season?"

Lila shook her head. "I doubt it."

"Well, I was thinking maybe since she's dating the production designer, she might know something," Nicola prodded.

Lila attempted to brush off the conversation. "If she does, she hasn't shared it with me."

"Perhaps you could ask her?" she urged, like a dog unwilling to release its bone.

Lila placed the Yorkie on the table. "I'm glad you brought Sweetpea in," she said with an exaggerated look of concern.

"Why? Do you think it could be something serious?"

Her diversion ploy did the trick. "Well, it's too early to tell."

The examination room was a bright, sterile space, with a stainless-steel table at its center where the Yorkie sat, her tiny paws shifting nervously. Lila, wearing a white lab coat and stethoscope around her neck, approached the little dog with a reassuring smile and gentle words. The Yorkie's eyes were wide and her ears perked as Lila's hand gently stroked her back, calming her.

"Let's check how you're feeling today," she said softly, carefully examining Sweetpea's abdomen for signs of bloating or discomfort. She palpated the belly in gentle, circular motions, observing the dog's reactions. The little dog squirmed slightly, indicating some discomfort, but allowed the examination to continue.

"See?" Nicola said anxiously. "I knew something was off."

Lila then took out a stethoscope and listened to the Yorkie's heart and lungs, noting there were no irregularities in the rhythm or breathing patterns.

Lila looked up from her exam. "Well, I think we're simply looking at bacon overload, and nothing more." She gave a knowing nod and explained that too much fatty food could upset a dog's stomach, leading to indigestion or pancreatitis in severe cases.

"Can you call and tell Wooster that?" Nicola suggested. "He won't listen to me."

"Tell you what—I'll write a script recommending a bland diet for the next few days, along with plenty of water to keep little Sweetpea hydrated. You can show that to Wooster, if you like." She also advised Nicola to monitor the dog's condition and return if symptoms like vomiting or diarrhea appeared. With a final pat on the Yorkie's head and a gentle scratch behind her ears, Lila concluded the examination, ensuring Nicola had all the information needed for a safe recovery.

As they made their way to the waiting room, Nicola turned with a mischievous smile. "By the way, have you heard the latest news?"

Lila sighed inwardly. "No, I haven't."

Nicola's eyes sparkled with excitement. "We have a new visitor in town. And not just any visitor—a celebrity."

That caught Lila's attention. "Really? Who is it?" she asked, her tone lifting with curiosity.

But Nicola was already moving toward the counter, her expression coy. Without breaking eye contact, she sat her dog on a nearby chair. Then she opened her purse, retrieved her wallet, and slid out a credit card.

"The woman is very well known in some circles," Nicola added. Her manicured nails tapped lightly on the counter as she waited for Lila to make out the invoice. The hint of a smile on her lips suggested she was enjoying this game of half-revealed secrets.

Next, she leaned across the counter. In a conspiratorial whisper, she finally spilled. "It's Roxie Steele."

Lila met her gaze. "Who?"

Nicola scooped Sweetpea into her arms. "Roxie Steele—the romance author!" Her voice carried a tinge of excitement. "She's been topping the charts for years."

She winked, her eyes gleaming with mischief. "Can you imagine? Our little town, hosting a bestselling author?"

Grabbing her clipboard off the counter, Lila moved for the cash register. "Never heard of her."

Nicola handed over her credit card. "Oh, c'mon. Every woman in America has heard of Roxie Steele. Her stories are..." She lowered her voice. "*Very* sexy. The kind you wouldn't want Camille reading."

Narrowing her eyes, Lila studied Nicola's overly enthusiastic expression. "Roxie Steele, huh? You read her books?" she asked casually, though she already had her suspicions.

Nicola rolled her eyes and waved a dismissive hand, her Yorkie shifting in her arms. "Me? Please, I don't have time for that kind of smut," she said, though her blush and sudden avoidance of eye contact suggested otherwise. "I'm too busy with more...refined reading material," she added, her voice trailing off with a slightly forced laugh.

Lila suppressed a smirk. It was clear as day that Nicola was lying. She could practically see the romance paperbacks stuffed in the woman's oversized designer handbag.

She shook her head lightly, pretending to believe her, but she knew that Nicola was the type to devour every steamy chapter when no one was watching.

"What is she doing in Thunder Mountain?" she asked.

"No one knows. All I heard was that she's staying out at the Teton Trails Guest Ranch."

Lila nodded absently, her mind already wandering to the idea of Roxie Steele lounging at Charlie Grace's Teton Trails Guest Ranch, perhaps drafting her next steamy bestseller. She glanced at the pile of veterinary journals on the bookshelf, suddenly feeling that they seemed drier than usual.

Maybe it wouldn't hurt to indulge in a little romantic escapism; after all, her love life had been as quiet as the town's abandoned mining shafts for far too long. A smutty novel could be just the thing to shake things up, even if it was just between the pages.

As Nicola sashayed out the door, her Yorkie in tow, Lila made a mental note to go online and check out Roxie Steele's latest work. If nothing else, it would give her something to gossip about with her next patient.

7

L ila tossed her purse on her kitchen counter, then bent and pulled off her shoes. It had been a long day.

She'd diagnosed a pregnant cat, treated a tiny dog with indigestion, vaccinated a litter of puppies, and treated Eddy Pisanelli's pet rat for pododermatitis, a bacterial infection on the skin of the feet, also known as bumblefoot. All before lunch.

The afternoon brought another series of pet ailments, thankfully nothing critical and all easily resolved.

Despite feeling exhausted, she was filled with satisfaction.

It had been her first day alone, holding down the fort in Doc Tillman's absence, and it felt wonderful. She didn't miss his constant critique, the way he would second-guess every decision she made.

A sense of accomplishment settled over her, grounding her in the certainty that this was the perfect profession for her. She didn't know what the future held, but the idea of being more than just a vet assistant to a crabby veterinarian gave her hope. The day had been hers, and she cherished the freedom it brought.

"Camille?" she called out. "I'm home."

That's when she noticed the note on the counter.

Mom, you were late, so I caught a ride to the ballgame. I'm going to stay over at Sheila's. Home in the morning. Love you.

Lila quickly glanced at the wall calendar. How had she forgotten it was Friday? She groaned out loud. How could she have blown off her daughter?

Thankfully, Camille was resourceful.

She quickly tapped out a message to her daughter apologizing and telling her she'd pick her up in the morning. "I promise," she added before adding a heart emoji.

She placed her phone on the counter and headed for the refrigerator hoping to find something to eat that didn't have to be cooked.

Her phone buzzed, diverting the plan.

Lila scooped up the phone and answered, "Hey, Charlie Grace. What's up?"

"I just talked to Capri. We're thinking of heading to the Jackson Hole Rodeo this weekend. Wanna go?"

She carried the phone to the refrigerator, opened the door, and scanned the nearly empty shelves. "What time?"

Goodness, she needed to go grocery shopping. What kind of mother left nothing for her kid to eat?

"Capri and I could pick you up midmorning. What do you say? It'll be fun."

Lila quickly calculated how much time it would take to pick up her daughter and stop by Western Drug and Grocery. "Okay, yeah. Midmorning should be fine."

"Great! See you then."

Lila clicked off her phone and pocketed it before heading for the pantry where she plucked out a nearly empty bag of chips, convincing herself that fried potatoes had nutritional value.

The following morning, Lila dragged herself from bed

when it was barely seven a.m. She immediately chastised herself for watching that last episode on Netflix, wishing she'd captured the extra time in sleep.

After showering and dressing, she tossed a load of laundry in the washing machine and mopped the kitchen floor before grabbing her keys and heading out to the car to pick up Camille. Before she drove a half mile, her phone buzzed with an incoming text from her daughter.

Mom, can I just stay with Sheila and go to the track meet this afternoon? Then, after that, we're all going out for pizza. I'll catch a ride home. Okay?

Lila smiled. She was happy her daughter had a busy social life, even if that meant seeing less of her. That was how it was supposed to be at her age.

"Sure, that's fine," she tapped out. She told her daughter of her plans to go to the rodeo in Jackson, and then she headed for the grocery store.

Camille would be graduating from high school next spring. The thought brought a wave of melancholy. Her graduation ceremony would be one of many life events Aaron would miss.

Inside Western Drug and Grocery, she grabbed a grocery cart, then tossed her purse in the place where she used to seat Camille when she was a toddler. She reached for the printed advertisements stacked in a rack to the right of the automatic door and scanned the front page as she pushed the cart toward the produce section where she grabbed a rare fresh pineapple.

She hoped Reva and Kellen were enjoying their honeymoon in Maui. A tiny pang of jealousy hit as she remembered a time she'd shown Aaron some travel magazine pictures of the Road to Hana. "Oh, let's go someday!"

A voice in her head rang out as clearly as if Aaron were right next to her.

"What's up with your fascination with Maui?"

She closed her eyes and remembered gazing up from the

pages of the magazine. "Are you crazy? It's only the most romantic place on earth," she'd so flippantly told her young husband.

Aaron playfully tugged at the sheet tucked around her bare waist. "Is that so?"

She quickly snatched the covering from his hands and secured it more tightly. "Yes, that's so. In fact, more people honeymoon in Hawaii than any other state in America." She held up the article as proof. "I can see why. Palm trees...beaches that stretch forever...sunsets to die for."

Aaron ran broad fingers through his sleep-tousled hair. "Yeah, you see—that's what I don't get. Why would we ever want to go to Hawaii when we live in the Tetons? This is heaven if you ask me."

She slammed the magazine against her new husband's chest. "I agree. That doesn't mean we can't go to Maui someday."

He laughed. "Okay, okay—look, I get it." His eyes sparkled when he'd said that. "Tell you what. When I get back from Afghanistan, we'll take a trip. I'll rub sunscreen all over that pretty back of yours, and we'll lay out on the beach for hours and soak up the scenery. How does that sound?"

Before she could respond, he pulled the magazine from her and tossed it to the floor, while at the same time lifting the sheet with his other hand.

She'd giggled as he buried his head against her skin. "Promise me," she said in a muffled voice. "Now. Promise. Or I'll—"

"Or you'll what?" His fingers dug into her sides, and he tickled, sending her entire torso into a fit of squirming. "Okay, I promise," he said.

"Careful, Aaron Bellamy. Because I intend to hold you to that," she shouted, laughing uncontrollably.

He immediately stopped tickling. Her new husband looked

at her then, his eyes boring into her soul. "And I promise I'll always love you."

"Hey, watch out!"

Lila looked up in horror, realizing in her reminiscing that she had neglected to watch where she was going and had nearly rammed her cart right into the balding store clerk.

"I'm so very sorry! Goodness, I almost ran into you."

Mr. Fouraker frowned in concern. "Lila, is everything all right? You seem a bit..."

"I'm fine," she hastily replied, her cheeks flushing with embarrassment. "Just daydreaming."

She picked up a head of crisp lettuce and dropped it into her basket, then added a bag of baby carrots with a gentle toss. The sound of the carrots rustling against the plastic broke the quiet tension. She glanced up at Mr. Fouraker, who still looked concerned, and gave him a quick wave and a tight-lipped smile. "Thanks, I'm good," she assured him, steering her cart toward the cereal aisle to avoid further questions.

The grocery store was abuzz with shoppers, the sound of rolling carts and distant conversations filling the air. Lila kept her head down, determined to focus on her list. She passed by the colorful cereal boxes, scanning the shelves for oat flakes. When she finally spotted her favorite brand, she reached for a box. As she placed the cereal in her basket, she heard a familiar voice.

She turned the corner into the next aisle, surprised to see Nicola Cavendish huddled and in deep conversation with a cluster of women. "Yes, that's what I said." Nicola's voice carried across the store, brimming with excitement. "A bestselling romance author. Staying right here in Thunder Mountain."

8

Lila hurried home with her groceries and had just put the last can in her pantry when the sound of a car engine drew her to the window. The girls had parked in her driveway and were heading up her sidewalk.

One of them knocked. Before she could answer, the front door opened, and her friends pushed their way inside.

"You ready to go?" Capri hollered.

Lila grabbed the jean jacket draped over her sofa, then reached for her purse. "Ready. I haven't been to Jackson in a while. This should be a blast."

As they set off, the drive was nothing less than spectacular. The landscape had transformed into a breathtaking palette of rich, vibrant colors. The aspens and cottonwoods that lined the river had turned a stunning shade of gold, their leaves shimmering in the crisp autumn breeze.

In the far distance, the Teton mountains rose dramatically from the valley floor, their sharp, rugged silhouettes etched against a crisp blue sky. Snow had begun to dust the highest summits, adding a touch of frosty white to the dramatic granite faces. Below the peaks, the slopes were adorned with vibrant bursts of fall foliage, where golden aspens and fiery orange sycamores created a striking contrast against the dark ever-greens and rock formations.

Tourists frequently confused the City of Jackson with the broader valley called Jackson Hole. Locals often used these terms interchangeably, which only added to the confusion for visitors trying to get their bearings. The nearby ski resort also shared the name Jackson Hole, further complicating matters.

The drive was filled with conversation, and Lila shared how busy she'd been lately. "But I'm loving it," she said. "I hate to admit this, but with Doc Tillman gone, I'm able to practice some veterinarian medicine without second-guessing every decision I make."

"Do you think this health scare will force his retirement?" Capri suggested.

Charlie Grace tapped her thumbs against the steering wheel and laughed. "Are you kidding? Doc retired? That will never happen."

Lila groaned from the front passenger seat. "That's what I fear. That I will be working in that man's shadow until I'm old and gray myself."

Her friends knew the clinic was her life. Her dream of becoming a full-fledged big animal vet would never allow her to resign and move on.

Capri huffed from the back seat. "Start your own clinic."

Lila shook her head. "You know I can't do that."

Capri's eyebrows lifted "Why not?"

Charlie Grace turned down the radio. "Money, for one. I can attest that starting your own business brings a plethora of financial issues."

Lila looked at her, a bit surprised. "But you had a great first season. The cabins were full nearly the entire summer."

"True," Charlie Grace admitted. "But there were expenses

and bank loan payments. My point is it's not easy to start your own business."

"It's not that hard," Capri argued. "I bought Grand Teton Whitewater Adventures against a lot of advice, and it's been a great run. Despite the high liability insurance premiums and getting all the permits." She leaned forward, straining against her seatbelt. "You should just go for it," she urged.

Lila shrugged. "Maybe someday."

They all exchanged glances in silence, knowing Lila could be stubborn when it came to change. Her someday would likely never come.

Lila dug in her purse for some gum, hoping to change the subject. "Well, sounds like you have a new guest out there at the ranch—a romance author?"

"How'd you hear the news so quickly," Charlie Grace asked. "She barely checked in two days ago."

"Nicola," they all said in unison, then laughed uncontrollably.

"Seriously, that new woman is a little strange," Charlie Grace told them.

Lila offered her friends the package of gum.

Capri took a stick. "How so?"

Charlie Grace shook her head. "No thanks. And to answer your question—first, I don't think Roxie Steele is her real name."

Lila shrugged. "That's not so uncommon. I hear authors use pen names all the time."

Capri blew a bubble with her gum and snapped it with a pop. "What makes you so sure Roxie isn't her real name?" she asked, her words slightly garbled as she chewed. She frowned as she pulled the wad from her mouth, opened the window, and tossed it. "How old was that gum?"

Ignoring her, Lila repeated Capri's question. "Why don't you think it's her real name?"

"She checked in under Roxie Steele and paid with a credit card with a business name. I couldn't quite make out her signature, but it wasn't Roxie Steele. It looked like Mary something."

Lila met her gaze. "Again, not that uncommon. I read somewhere that a lot of authors publish their own work these days. They make more money and have more control."

Capri giggled from the back seat. "Well, that makes sense. I heard she writes smut."

"Meaning?" Lila asked.

"Meaning she doesn't have to answer to anyone but herself. She can take whatever—uh, liberties—she wants to with her stories." She grinned. "If you know what I'm getting at."

Charlie Grace glanced at Capri in the rearview mirror. "She dared to leave some of those books on the coffee table inside the lodge. I'm no prude, but let's just say Aunt Mo saw the covers and quickly hid them."

Lila took up the argument. "Okay, so she writes suggestive stories."

"Smut," Capri repeated.

Lila sighed with impatience. "Like I was saying, that might not be the fare most ladies in Thunder Mountain would be seen reading, but it's a free country. People can read what they want, right?"

"Tell that to Pastor Pete," Charlie Grace suggested.

"And to Aunt Mo," Capri added.

Charlie Grace raised a hand from the wheel and tucked a stray piece of hair behind her ear. "I'm afraid that's not all. She dresses a lot like those women on her book covers. Roxie Steele is very proud of her cleavage. And get this, the woman made a pass at my dad."

Lila's eyebrows lifted. "At Clancy?"

Charlie Grace visibly winced. "Yeah, she ran her fingers along his back as she walked behind him at the dinner table and suggested he take her for a ride sometime." Her face twisted with disgust. "And I don't think she meant on his wheelchair."

"Gross." Lila wrinkled her nose.

"Seriously," Charlie Grace agreed. "And she did it right in front of my daughter."

"That's double nasty," Capri chimed in.

As they drove closer to town, ranches and wooden fences dotted their route. To the left, a paved path with occasional cyclists and pedestrians ran parallel to the highway. To the right, off in the distance, was the Jackson Hole Airport. Eventually, the familiar "Welcome to Jackson" sign appeared.

A brief silence settled in the car until Lila spoke up. "Well, we'll see what comes of Roxie Steele's visit. But it looks like Nicola Cavendish has finally met her match in the inappropriate department."

The others nodded in quick agreement.

"You can say that again," Capri said, laughing.

9

Lila stepped out of the vehicle, her boots sinking slightly into the soft dirt of the Jackson Hole Rodeo grounds. The afternoon sun cast long shadows across the arena, where rows of weathered bleachers buzzed with excited spectators. The air was thick with the scent of hot dogs and popcorn mixed with the unmistakable musk of livestock.

"Wow, look at the crowd," she said.

Capri looped her arm through Lila's as they walked toward the entrance. "Looks like fun!"

"Smells like manure," Charlie Grace added with a laugh, her eyes scanning the colorful banners flapping in the breeze.

They passed through the gates, and immediately, the chaotic noise of the rodeo engulfed them—the announcer's booming voice over the loudspeakers, children shouting, and the clatter of hooves in the distance. Music blared from hidden speakers, as several men on horses maneuvered around the arena.

"Look at that, Lila! He's massive!" Charlie Grace pointed to the left, where a large bull was being corralled by a few cowboys.

"Yeah, wouldn't want to be on the receiving end of that," Lila replied, squinting against the sun. "Let's find a good spot before the bull riding starts."

They navigated through groups of people, the ground vibrating underfoot with the energy of the event. The trio found seats high up in the bleachers, giving them a perfect view of the arena.

"This is going to be amazing," Capri murmured, her eyes wide as she took in the scene. "I love rodeos."

"You love the cowboys," Charlie Grace teased.

"It's something, isn't it?" Capri responded, her voice tinged with teasing. "Men in tight jeans."

As they settled in, the smell of sawdust became more pronounced, mixing with the tangy scent of barbecue from a nearby vendor.

The announcer's voice boomed through the loudspeakers, inviting everyone to stand for the opening ceremony. The arena immediately quieted down, anticipation hanging in the air.

Suddenly, the gates swung open, and a female rider burst into the arena at a gallop, carrying the United States flag. The flag billowed magnificently behind her as she guided her horse in a swift, graceful lap around the perimeter of the arena. The horse, a stunning specimen with a glossy coat, moved with precision and pride, its hooves kicking up clouds of dust in perfect rhythm.

The crowd immediately placed their hands over hearts, some holding their cowboy hats against their chests, as the rider directed her horse through elegant loops and swift turns, showcasing both the animal's training and her own riding prowess. The flag waved dramatically, catching the light of the afternoon sun.

Lila joined the crowd as everyone sang the national anthem. To her right, a gray-haired man bellowed the words as tears formed in his eyes. She nudged Charlie Grace with her elbow and pointed him out.

Charlie Grace leaned close. "I never tire of this part."

As the rider completed the circuit around the arena, she slowed her horse to a trot, passing in front of the grandstand where the cheers crescendo. With one final salute—a tip of her hat—the rider exited through the gates, leaving a lasting impression as the rodeo officially began.

"Did I ever tell you guys about the year Camille was bound and determined she wanted to grow up and be a cowgirl? She begged for a horse," Lila told them. "Which I couldn't afford, of course."

Charlie Grace chuckled. "I remember. So, you brought her out to the ranch and let her ride. For hours."

"And hours," Lila said, completing her friend's comment. "Thank goodness she grew out of that phase. It wasn't long before she turned in her cowboy hat and rodeo dreams for that old guitar Clancy gave her. She stood on the back patio and plunked that thing, pretending to be a music star."

"The next Reba McEntire?" Charlie Grace asked.

Lila shook her head. "Avril Lavigne."

They turned their attention to the gate as a rider entered the arena. The cowgirl quickly accelerated her horse towards the first of three barrels arranged in a triangular pattern. Approaching the first barrel, she expertly pulled on the reins, guiding her horse into a sharp, tight turn around the barrel. The horse pivoted on its hind legs, almost hugging the barrel with its body.

Next, the rider urged her horse into a swift sprint towards the second barrel. As they reached it, she leaned deeply into the turn, her body nearly parallel to the ground, maintaining a delicate balance as her horse executed another rapid, close turn. The precision required was immense, as any misstep could knock over the barrel, resulting in penalties.

With two barrels done, they dashed towards the third, the dust kicking up beneath the horse's hooves. The final turn mirrored the first two, but with added urgency, as this marked the final stretch. The rider and her horse whipped around the third barrel with impressive coordination and burst toward the finish line in a full, exhilarating sprint.

The crowd cheered.

Several more barrel racers made their runs. When the event finished, Charlie Grace pointed in the direction of the concession stand. "You girls want a hot dog?"

"Yes, I'm starving." Capri dug in her back pocket for her wallet.

Charlie Grace shook her head. "I got it." She turned to Lila. "You want something?"

"I'd donate my next child for something cold to drink."

That brought a laugh from Capri. "By the way, don't bother getting a slice of their pizza. Last year, Reva said it tasted like a Western Horsemen catalog."

"Noted," Charlie Grace said, descending the stairs.

Capri held up a finger. "Wait, I'll come, too. You can't carry all that by yourself." She raced to follow her friend, leaving Lila alone in the stands.

The first bull rider burst into the arena, clinging to a twisting, bucking beast. The crowd roared, and she joined in, swept up in the excitement.

"Go! Hold tight!" she shouted, standing up, her hands clenched in excitement.

"Eight seconds, that's all he needs," the gray-haired man next to her explained, his eyes fixed on the rider.

The buzzer sounded, and the rider was thrown off, landing in the dirt with a thud that drew a collective gasp from the spectators. Two rodeo clowns rushed to his side, but he got up, dusted himself off, and raised his hat to the cheering crowd.

Lila winced sympathetically. "That's got to hurt."

"Yeah, but you gotta admire the courage," the old man replied, his admiration evident as he lifted his worn cowboy hat and wiped his brow with his sleeve.

Lila leaned forward, absorbing the sights and sounds of the rodeo as the next rider prepared for his turn.

Lila's heart pounded in sync with the crowd's rising excitement as a bull, its muscles rippling under a sleek coat, charged into the arena. The rider, a figure of sheer determination, clung on for dear life, his hand wrapped tight in the rope, his body swaying with each violent jerk of the bull.

She felt herself drawn into the visceral struggle between man and beast, her hands clutching the bleacher's edge. The air was electric, the crowd's cheers swelling into a thunderous crescendo, echoing the fury of the ride.

Suddenly, the bull stumbled. A collective gasp sliced through the noise. Lila watched, heart in her throat, as the rider was thrown clear, rolling away from the thrashing bull, unharmed yet shaken. The bull, however, was not so fortunate; it limped, favoring one leg, pain evident in its movements.

The arena fell into a concerned hush, the excitement quickly turning to worry. Murmurs of concern rippled through the stands, and Lila found herself whispering hopes for its recovery.

Claims that rodeo animal injuries were common were debunked by extensive studies. PRCA rodeos had a high safety rating with less than one percent of livestock exposures resulting in any form of injury. Still, there were those rare occasions, and this appeared to be one of them.

The bull stumbled and went down, falling hard into the dirt. The cowboy rushed across the arena in the direction of the chutes. "We need a vet," he shouted.

Lila bolted up from her seat. "I have to help!"

Without thinking the decision through, Lila bolted from her seat and rushed down the stands, determined to help. She raced for the gate, leaped over the barrier, and then made her way to the injured animal, now being tended to by a small group of rodeo staff. "I'm Doc Tillman's vet assistant—in Thunder Mountain," she declared upon approach. "Let me help."

Never did she stop to consider how absurd her offer might appear to the men gathered. Nor did she consider that the bull might rise at any moment and thrash around, perhaps injuring her and the others.

One of the men extended a hand. "I'm Bill—the official rodeo vet. Glad for the assistance." He motioned to the others. "Stand back. Safety first."

He gestured towards a nearby bag. "Grab that bottle of ace and a syringe."

Lila complied and did as she was instructed. Without being asked, she began filling the syringe with liquid. "How much acepromazine?"

Bill gave her an appreciative nod. "Start small," he advised, specifying the number of milliliters. "We can always administer more if needed."

Once the tranquilizer had been administered, Lila knelt by the bull, watching as Bill assessed its injury—an ankle that was visibly swelling. She looked up to coordinate with Bill on whether he might need a nose twitch for further restraint when a guy clad in jeans and a blue button-down shirt, stepped in front of her, blocking her view.

Lila firmly rose to her feet. "Excuse me."

He turned his back to her as he bent and slid his hand down the injured leg. "I doubt it's broken. Just needs a little ice and rest."

Lila stepped forward, insistent. "The bull needs to be stabilized before moving. We should strap his leg and check for fractures with a portable X-ray."

The intruder held up open palms, clearly annoyed. "That's overkill, in my opinion. But sure, X-ray it."

He glared at Lila before turning this attention to Bill. "Just offering my opinion. I'm a certified large animal vet."

"Look, we don't have time for egos." Her voice remained steady and commanding as she looked him directly in the eyes. "This animal is in pain."

Bill tilted his head in Lila's direction. "I'm afraid I have to side with her. We can't assume the leg's not broken. But we're going to have to take the animal off-site for the X-ray since we don't have a portable at our disposal."

The guy rubbed at his right ear lobe and begrudgingly stepped aside. Lila moved back to the bull, carefully strapping its leg with the help of the rodeo staff.

Once the sedated animal was loaded into a waiting hauler, she turned to find the guy was gone. Good riddance, she thought as she headed back to the stands.

"Wow! What was the deal down there?" Charlie Grace asked as she handed Lila a hot dog. "Hope your food is not cold."

Lila gave them a brief rundown of what had occurred in the arena. "The bull likely suffered a transverse fracture. Hard to diagnose because they tend to be stable breaks. If an X-ray confirms my suspicion, with proper treatment, the animal should be fine."

"Ooh...listen to you, talking all professional and veterinarian-like." Capri teased as she unwrapped a straw and shoved it into her plastic cup of Coca-Cola. "So, who was that hot guy down there?"

Lila shrugged. "I don't know. Some veterinarian. Probably a tourist here on vacation. But he was an a..." She stopped mid-sentence. "He was a jerk." She peeled the wrapping from her hot dog and took a bite. "Argued against my assessment—which by the way, the rodeo vet agreed with."

Capri chuckled. "Never bet against Lila when it comes to animals."

Charlie Graced nodded in agreement. "Or anything else, really."

10

A week later, Reva and Kellen arrived home from their extended honeymoon trip to Maui. Lila couldn't help but feel a surge of excitement tinged with a hint of envy at the thought of the adventures they must have had. She stood at Reva's door with Charlie Grace and Capri, eager to hear all about their vacation.

"Maybe we should've texted before just dropping in," Charlie Grace warned. "Reva is a married woman now."

"What? You think we'll catch Kellen in his underwear?" Capri laughed. "He'll learn."

Lila held her breath as Capri knocked. "Well, true...but we might be a bit much for the poor man. I mean, we're a lot to get used to."

Capri knocked again. "Like I said, he'll adjust."

The door opened and Reva stood there, looking surprised to see them. Nonetheless, her eyes brightened. "Oh, my goodness! I've missed you girls." She scooped them into a group hug. "Come in." She motioned them inside.

"So, was it as wonderful as you hoped?" Charlie Grace asked.

"The honeymoon trip, not the..." Lila cleared her throat and lowered her voice. "You know."

Reva playfully slapped her friend's shoulder. "Both were wonderful." The corners of her mouth lifted in a sly smile.

Lila peeled off her denim jacket and placed it over the back of a chair. "We can't wait to hear all about it."

"Obviously," came Reva's reply. "Let me get you girls a cup of coffee and then I'll tell you everything."

"Everything?" Capri teased.

"Not everything," a man's voice answered.

Kellen walked toward them from down the hallway, smiling. He held little Lucan in his arms.

"I—I didn't mean that," Capri stammered. They all knew she was lying between her teeth, so she grinned. "You can tell us later, Reva." She winked at her friend.

They all laughed. Even Lucan joined in while waving his stuffed turtle in the air.

Kellen walked barefoot to the refrigerator and pulled the door open. "Well, I guess I'll let my new wife have some time with her friends." He retrieved a bottle of apple juice and a toddler's sippy cup from the cupboard. "We'll be on the deck if you need us." He planted a kiss on Reva's cheek and granted another wide smile to the rest of them before heading outside.

Reva motioned them to the sofa. "Sit. Let me get the coffee, and I'll join you. I can't wait to tell you all about our romantic trip."

She returned minutes later with a large tray filled with mugs of steaming coffee, a plate of donuts, and a plate of sliced pineapple. "There's more coffee in the carafe," she told them, pointing to the silver container on the tray.

Capri grabbed a donut that was covered in powdered sugar. "Oh, thank goodness. I'm starved."

When the others gave her a look, she frowned. "What? I didn't eat breakfast."

Charlie Grace waved her off and turned to Reva. "Was the trip everything you hoped? Did you get to connect with Tom and Ava? Did you get to tour Pali Maui?"

Reva wrapped both hands around her steaming mug. "Yes... to everything." She took a quick sip before continuing. "Pali Maui was amazing. I'd never been on a pineapple plantation. We had a private tour. Did you know pineapples take up to twenty-four months from propagation to fruit?"

"That's what Ava told us when she was visiting out at Teton Trails. I couldn't believe it took that long." Charlie Grace took a piece of pineapple and slipped it in her mouth. Juice escaped the corners of her mouth as she chewed. "This is delicious!" she said, grabbing for a napkin.

Reva nodded in agreement. "The Pali Maui pineapples are the sweetest I've ever tasted."

"Did you go to a luau?" Capri asked.

"We did! Ava's best friend, Alani, runs one of the most popular on the island. We got to experience the whole shebang. Kalua pork cooked in a pit. Huli huli chicken. Lomi lomi." She chuckled. "We didn't care for the poi. Tasted like that paste we used in elementary school."

Charlie Grace wrinkled her nose. "Sounds awful. Did you go snorkeling?"

Reva's eyes lit up. "That might have been my favorite part. The multi-colored fish under the water—" She sighed. "It was just like I dreamed. Oh, and the turtles. You're warned not to touch them, but they swim right up to you under the water." She leaned back into the sofa cushion. "We truly had the best time."

Capri took a sip from her mug. "We should all plan a trip and go sometime. A girl's getaway," she suggested.

A smile nipped at the corners of Charlie Grace's lips. "Good luck finding a time when we can all slip away from our responsibilities."

Capri gave her a look. "Party pooper."

Reva turned to Charlie Grace. "By the way, Ava and Tom both said to tell you hello. They were effusive in their praise of the time they spent at Teton Trails. Ava told me she hopes to bring her family for Christmas in the future. Her grandchildren have never seen snow."

"That would be wonderful," Charlie Grace said. "I hope she does. From what I hear, the Briscoes are an amazing bunch." She sighed. "Until then, I'll simply attend to our newest guest, Roxie Steele. She's a handful."

"Who?" Reva asked.

The others quickly filled her in on the hot romance author and her antics. "She's like a cougar on the prowl," Charlie Grace told them. "Seriously."

Capri laughed. "I guess she visited the bank the other day wearing a low-cut blouse that left Wooster Cavendish's eyes wider than a barn owl's at midnight. I wouldn't want to be her if Nicola learns of it. Friend or foe—she'll take her out."

"Yeah." Lila scrunched her face. "I wouldn't want to be in the middle of that catfight."

Reva shook her head. "I'm away for only a couple of weeks and the town blows up with trouble." She directed her attention to Lila. "I hear you've done a wonderful job filling in for Doc Tillman while he's been away."

Charlie Grace eyed the platter and reached for another piece of pineapple. "Everyone in town is singing her praises. Even Nicola. She says you took excellent care of Sweetpea."

"That's high praise," Capri offered.

"Not only that," Charlie Grace added. "But Lila assisted when a bull suffered an injury at the Jackson Hole Rodeo last weekend. She was amazing."

Capri agreed. "We're proud of our girl."

Lila blushed. "Well, thank you. Some days I wonder if all the work will ever pay off."

"Sure it will," Reva reached and patted her arm. "You'll get your large animal certificate, and the world will be your oyster."

"We live in the mountains," Lila reminded. "Not many oysters here except the Rocky Mountain kind. Likewise, there aren't a lot of opportunities for me to practice unless I were to move. That's out of the question," she said vehemently. "And I'm not sure Doc will be open to sharing his practice with another vet. He complains there isn't enough revenue now, and that he's barely able to keep the doors open."

Reva picked up a napkin and wiped up some coffee that had dribbled onto the tray. "That's because he's a terrible financial manager."

"Well, Doc Tillman would be a fool not to promote you and utilize your skills," Charlie Grace offered. "Besides, he has to retire someday."

Reva picked up the carafe and refilled her mug. "After that health scare, it might be sooner than later."

Lila held her mug up for a refill, her thoughts wandering to a future where she might step into Doc Tillman's well-worn shoes. The very idea of taking over his role in Thunder Mountain filled her with an electric mix of excitement and nerves. Though she wished no ill will on the beloved vet, she couldn't help but secretly hope for the day he would decide to retire, leaving a space for her to fulfill her dream. Every day, with each animal she treated, Lila felt herself preparing for that coveted role, dreaming of the day she could serve the community she loved in a way that truly resonated with her deepest aspirations.

They heard footsteps and Kellen appeared clutching Lucan. "Sorry to interrupt, ladies. But Little Man has sprouted a leak." He pointed to the toddler's wet pants.

Reva quickly lifted from her place on the sofa. "Here, I'll take him." She plucked Lucan from Kellen's arms, apologizing to her guests as she followed her husband and headed for the hallway leading to the nursery, calling over her shoulder, "We're still working on the potty-training thing. I'll be right back."

As the others returned to their conversation, Lila found herself thinking about what her friends had said earlier. They were right. Doc Tillman had to retire at some point.

The road ahead might be long, with its own set of challenges and uncertainties, but the thought of eventually stepping into Doc Tillman's role sparked a hopeful light within her.

The incident at the rodeo had proven she had the skills necessary to take over the clinic.

For now, she would continue to learn, to care for her neighbors and their animals, and to wait patiently. Someday, the dream she was holding would come true.

When that time came, she was determined to be ready.

11

T he tantalizing aroma of bacon coaxed Lila from her bed. After throwing off her covers, she headed for the shower. While she dressed, she took a quick mental inventory of the day ahead of her—Doc Tillman's first day back at the clinic.

It was Monday, and they had no overnight patients at the clinic, no boarders.

The first appointment wasn't until after lunch. She'd been scheduled to go out to Teton Trails later in the afternoon to check on one of Charlie Grace's trail horses, thought to have an infected abscess on its leg.

Things had remained busy in Doc's absence. She hoped to show him the clinic had been left in good hands.

Downstairs, she headed for the kitchen to find Camille standing at the stove with a spatula in her hand. "Morning, Mom."

"Well, what's this?" Lila asked, peeking over her daughter's shoulder.

"I made breakfast."

"I see that." Lila had noticed a growing maturity in her daughter lately—a glimpse of the woman she would become. She liked what she saw. "Thank you, honey. I'm starving."

While she didn't have time, she sat and let her daughter bring her a plate filled with bacon, scrambled eggs, and toast.

"I know you're in a hurry," Camille said. "So, eat and I'll clean up."

Lila swelled with pride. "That's so thoughtful. I need to get to the clinic this morning."

"Yeah, 'cuz Doc's back, right?"

"He is," Lila confirmed. She scooped a bite of eggs. "I need to bring him up to speed on everything."

After finishing her food, Lila kissed her daughter's cheek. "Thanks again, honey. Gotta go."

Camille shooed her out the door but before she reached her car, she called her back. "Mom. You forgot your keys." She dangled the set from her fingers.

Lila scrambled back and hooked them over her own finger. "Ugh. My mind this morning."

Minutes later, as she steered her car down the winding roads toward the vet clinic, her mind continued to buzz with the imminent return of Doc Tillman. Emotions tangled within her, an unease she grappled to admit.

She was grateful for her job. But her boss's condescending demeanor always managed to chip away at her confidence. His arrival meant enduring his patronizing remarks and belittling attitude, stirring up feelings of frustration and inadequacy she'd rather keep buried.

Through the windshield, the early autumn morning unfolded like a scene from a picture-perfect movie. The sunlight danced upon the foliage lining the river outside of town, painting the landscape in hues of amber and gold. Lila couldn't help but be captivated by the serene beauty surrounding her, even as her thoughts continued to drift back to Doc's return.

As Lila's car approached the outskirts of town, Thunder Mountain came into view. The quaint charm of the town enveloped her as she drove along the main street. Wooden sidewalks lined with rustic storefronts greeted her, each building adorned with awnings. Whisky barrel planters brimming with vibrant mums and trailing bright green potato vines added bursts of color to the scene, creating a picturesque tableau against the backdrop of the mountainous landscape. The sight filled Lila with a sense of nostalgia, reminding her of the simplicity and beauty of small-town life.

She offered warm smiles and waves to familiar faces of townspeople beginning their day. Barb Miller and Patty Guerard stood at the front of their tiny clothing store, Apricot Lane, hanging a sale sign on their front window offering forty percent off summer items. Albie Barton was busy unlocking the door leading into the *Thunder Mountain Gazette* office. Dorothy Vaughn stood at the open door of Bear Country Gifts and waved as Lila passed.

Lila took a deep breath as she slowed at the intersection leading to the vet clinic. "Well, here goes," she said out loud while pulling into the gravel parking lot minutes later.

Doc Tillman was in the back. "Morning," he said, in a singsong voice Lila barely recognized. "How are you this fine day, Lila?"

She tried hard not to frown. *Who was this man, and where had her boss gone?*

"Good morning," she said tentatively while pushing her purse and sack lunch into a waiting cubby. "Glad to have you back, Doc."

"Glad to be back," he told her. "But I have to say, I enjoyed my time away. I hate to admit Winnie was right, but a vacation was just what we needed." His face broke into a wide smile. "We met up with Derek and his family."

His son lived in Florida with his wife and three little children, all elementary-aged. Winnie adored her grandchildren and often lamented she didn't see them enough.

She once told Lila that Derek had an important job at the Kennedy Space Center. He was an engineer and couldn't get away but for two weeks a year. That time was split with seeing his wife's family who lived in upstate New York.

Lila slipped her arms into her white lab coat and clipped on her name tag. "Oh? How is your son?"

"He's great. For the first time in a long while, we had a chance to catch up. And those children...well, I'll have you know this ole grandpa rode on It's a Small World with those little girls."

Lila's eyes widened with surprise. "You did?"

Doc nodded with enthusiasm. "I sure did. And the Matterhorn, the spinning teacups, and we toured Sleeping Beauty's Castle. Oh, and did you know there's a Big Thunder Mountain Railroad? Same name as our town." He chuckled. "Who knew?"

She listened with rapt interest. This was a side of Doc Tillman she'd never seen. His entire demeanor was different. His eyes sparkled with a newfound excitement, and a genuine smile lit up his face as he recounted his adventures.

Lila couldn't help but feel a twinge of awe at the transformation before her. Gone was the condescending tone and aloof demeanor she had grown accustomed to—in its place was a warmth and openness she hadn't expected from Doc Tillman. As she gazed into his eyes, she saw a glimmer of joy and passion that she had never witnessed before. It was as if her boss had shed his old self and emerged anew, revealing a side of him she had never known existed.

"Well, that's good to hear, Doc. So glad you had a good time."

The phone buzzed in his pocket, and he plucked it out. He looked at the tiny screen and smiled. "Well, hello sweetheart," he answered, beaming.

Lila continued to listen, still amazed at the profound change in Doc.

"Yes, Winnie. Yes, dear. No, I haven't told her yet." He smiled as he listened. "Okay, yeah. I'll try to be home early. I love you, too." He whispered something then and chuckled. "I look forward to it."

Doc pocketed his phone and opened his mouth. "We have something we need to discuss," he told her.

Suddenly, they heard the front office door open. "Doc! Come quick!"

Both Doc and Lila raced into the waiting room to find Earl Dunlop rushing toward them cradling his ginger-colored kitty in his arms.

"Fluffy is sick again, Doc!" Earl announced, his voice filled with concern as he made his way to the front counter.

Doc Tillman gently pushed Lila aside, his eyebrows knit with worry. "Here, give Fluffy to me."

Earl shifted uncomfortably and quickly did as he was told. "Doc, you have to do something." He placed his precious pet into Doc's waiting hands.

Lila's heart dropped as she glanced between the frantic man and his lethargic cat. "Wait here, Earl."

She followed her boss to the treatment area in the back of the clinic.

Doc Tillman's commitment to saving every creature was evident in his every action. With a gentle touch and a determined spirit, he worked tirelessly to heal the beloved pets of their town, including Earl's cat, Fluffy.

Despite his best efforts, there were moments when the harsh reality of veterinary care was painfully clear. Even given Doc's expertise and compassion, he couldn't save them all.

Each loss weighed heavily on him, casting a somber shadow over his demeanor. In those moments, she couldn't help but admire his dedication, even as he faced the heart-wrenching truth that not every animal could be saved.

Sadly, when Doc looked up at her, she knew.

This was one of those cases.

12

Fluffy's funeral was held that evening in Earl's backyard. Several townspeople showed up in support of the large, gruff man who ran the county snow removal fleet. He was their friend, and he was broken at the loss of his pet.

Lila approached Earl, gently patting his arm. "You did everything you could, Earl. Fluffy knew she was loved."

Albie, standing nearby, chimed in with a reassuring nod. "That's right, Earl. You gave that kitty a good life."

Pastor Pete stepped forward, offering a comforting hand on Earl's shoulder. "Fluffy was more than just a pet, Earl. She was family. And remember, in the eyes of the Lord, all creatures great and small find their way to heaven."

Earl nodded, his eyes misty with emotion. "Thanks, Pastor Pete. Means a lot."

Meanwhile, the Knit Wits had taken charge of the food, and they certainly didn't disappoint. As friends gathered in Earl's backyard, they were greeted with a sumptuous spread of home-made dishes. The air was filled with the tantalizing aroma of slow-cooked brisket, savory potato side dishes, and freshly baked bread. There were casseroles overflowing with cheesy goodness, bowls of steaming soup, and platters of delectable desserts. It was a true feast, a testament to the Knit Wits' culinary prowess and their unwavering support for their grieving friend.

Oma Griffith passed a plate to Earl. "Honey, eat something."

He wiped at the corner of his eyes and took the plate, thanking her. He loaded it with mounds of food. Minutes later, he was seen eating like he hadn't had a meal in days.

It wasn't until the following morning that Lila remembered what Doc had said to his wife on the phone before Earl had shown up with his sick pet.

She finished unpacking a box of antibiotics and placed the last bottle on the shelf. "Doc, what did you mean when you said you had something to tell me?"

"What?"

"When you were on the phone with Winnie. You said you hadn't told me yet."

Doc pivoted, his hands sliding into the pockets of his lab coat. "That's right. We were interrupted yesterday." Lila's heart raced with anticipation. She leaned in, eager. "What were you going to tell me?"

Doc half sat on the stainless-steel examination table, his arms now folded in front of him. "Well, it's like this. Winnie has been hounding me for a long time to slow down. She wants to travel. We both wish to spend more time with our son and his family."

He looked at her and Lila wondered if he could see her heart pounding. Surely, the intense hammering was visible through her lab coat. She swallowed and clasped together sweaty hands, waiting for him to continue.

Outside the window, a pickup pulled into a parking space and stopped, a lone star matching the Texas license plates visible in the rear window. The polished deep blue exterior of the pickup truck gleamed in the sunlight, its chrome accents shimmering with brilliance.

Doc stood. "Oh, looks like he's here."

"Who's here?" Lila asked, frowning. Why did they get interrupted every time Doc was about to share his news? News she suspected was announcing his retirement. News that could change her life.

Doc motioned for her to follow him outside.

Lila's heart skipped a beat as she trailed after Doc, her mind racing. Who was this guy?

As they stepped out onto the porch, the scene of freshly cut grass and the distant promise of rain hung in the air. Lila squinted against the sunlight, her gaze landing on the figure emerging from the pickup truck. Tall and broad-shouldered, he moved with a confidence that demanded attention.

"Lila," Doc began, his voice tinged with a hint of excitement. "Meet Whit Calloway."

The name rolled off Doc's tongue with a sense of significance that sent a shiver down Lila's spine as she stepped forward.

Suddenly, her heart jumped a beat.

It was him. The guy from the rodeo.

She swallowed against the dryness collecting in the back of her throat. "Whit," she echoed, her voice barely above a whisper.

He approached with a casual swagger, a pompous grin playing at the corners of his lips as he recognized her. "Nice to see you again," he drawled, his words sending a jolt of electricity through the air.

The look in his eyes told her his statement wasn't exactly genuine.

Lila's mind raced as she struggled to maintain her composure. A palpable tension hung in the air, reminiscent of their earlier encounter in that arena.

Doc cleared his throat, a serious look settling over his features as he observed the charged silence between Lila and Whit. "So, you two have met before?"

Lila managed a nod, her thoughts in turmoil. What was happening? Why was this guy here?

"We met briefly the other night." Whit's eyes met Lila's. "In Jackson."

"Well, I've got some news," Doc continued, his gaze shifting between the two of them. "I'm planning on retiring soon. Been thinking about it for a while. After my little heart incident, both Winnie and I agree it's time."

Doc sighed, looking genuinely pained. "Whit, give us a moment?"

Whit leaned against his truck and nodded.

Doc took Lila's elbow and guided her out of earshot of Whit.

Her heart, already unsteady, now acted like it was the drummer in the town's Fourth of July parade.

Doc adjusted his glasses against the glare of the late morning sun. "Now, Lila, I know you've been with me for years and you've put your heart into this clinic. I always appreciated that," he said, his voice steady yet carrying an undertone of regret.

Lila nodded, the muscles in her jaw tightening. She sensed something was coming, something she might not like.

"But—" Doc continued, pausing to choose his words carefully. "After a lot of thought, and considering my health, Winnie and I have decided it would be best if I retire sooner rather than later." He hesitated, glancing in the direction of Whit who stood at a distance, leaning against his truck with a self-assured smile. "I've asked Whit Calloway to take over the clinic."

The world seemed to freeze around Lila. The chirping of the birds, the rustle of the leaves in the breeze, everything fell away into a stifling silence. She stared at Doc, her heart pounding furiously, her mind refusing to accept the words she just heard.

"But...I thought—I mean, I've been here..." Her words trailed off into nothingness, her throat constricted with a mix of disbelief and betrayal.

Lila felt a surge of anger, her face flushing with heat. "You can't be serious, Doc," she said, her voice cracking. "He's not even qualified." She told him what happened at the rodeo.

"It's not that uncommon for veterinarians to have difference approaches when treating animals," Doc told her. "Whit Calloway comes highly recommended. Believe me, I checked this guy out carefully, and he'll be a great fit for this community. Regardless of who is in charge, I think you'll come to respect one another and work as a team."

What could she say to that? Yes, vets could disagree, but this guy held an arrogance—a reluctance to consider other opinions. He was trouble. She could sense it.

"Lila, I know this is hard to hear. I wouldn't make this decision if I didn't believe it was the best for the clinic. Whit has the skills and the know-how. He's had a lot of experience, and he can bring a lot to the table. That, and he's fully licensed and ready to take over."

"But you know I'll have my certificate soon, Doc. This clinic is everything I've worked for." Lila's voice was thick with emotion, her eyes glistening with unshed tears.

She couldn't believe that her mentor, the man she'd worked under for so many years, would choose a stranger over her. Yes, Doc could be critical—but she always suspected her boss's gruff ways might simply be him grooming her to take over someday. She never suspected he might do otherwise.

Her dream of taking over the clinic, of serving the community she loved, seemed to shatter right in front of her.

Doc placed a hand on her shoulder, his touch no longer comforting but heavy, laden with finality. "I'm sorry, Lila. I truly am. But given my health scare, Winnie and I don't want to wait. Whit assures me you'll have plenty of opportunity for advancement here. I made sure of that."

Despite Doc's guarantee, they both knew there was little opportunity for advancement in such a small clinic. Yet what choice did she have? It's not like she could quit. Not unless she was willing to walk away from veterinarian medicine and do something else.

Lila's mind swirled with a tumult of thoughts and feelings. Betrayed, sidelined, and utterly heartbroken, she turned and walked away, leaving Doc behind, along with Whit who still leaned against his truck with that smug smile.

As she stepped off the porch, the fresh scent of the grass seemed to mock her, a bitter reminder of the future she thought she was building. Now, all that lay ahead was uncertainty and the daunting task of confronting the man she had immediately loathed yet was now forced to acknowledge as her new boss.

13

C apri hated going to the bank. In fact, there was a myriad of mundane business chores associated with running Grand Teton Whitewater Adventures that she detested. Keeping books, tax preparation, marketing...those activities were as dull as dishwater.

Her passion was the local rivers and battling their powerful currents. Even more, she loved sharing the adventure with her customers and seeing them discover their own strength and tenacity. Every rapid they mastered not only boosted their confidence but also deepened their appreciation for the untamed beauty and formidable power of the Class II and III rapids on the Snake River and the renowned Hoback—waterways celebrated by whitewater enthusiasts far and wide.

Unfortunately, that exhilaration was tempered with this other stuff. When you were a business owner, some tasks simply landed on your plate and had to be done.

Capri pushed open the heavy, glass door of Thunder Mountain Savings and Loan, a quaint bank nestled in the heart of their small mountain town. Inside, the interior smelled faintly of pine and old paper, a testament to its rustic charm. Wooden beams supported the ceiling, and the walls were adorned with historic black and white photos of the town. Across the lobby, a few elderly locals were seated in creaky chairs, filling out deposit slips with slow, careful strokes.

She spotted Wooster Cavendish, the bank manager, a portly man with a perpetually loosened tie at his collar, standing behind a polished pine wood counter, shuffling papers. "Morning, Wooster!" Capri called out as she passed.

Wooster looked up, his expression softening into a smile. "Ah, Capri! Good to see you. Trust the river's been kind this season?"

"Never better!" she replied, heading towards the teller windows.

Thelma DeRosier peered at her from behind thick, coke-bottle glasses that magnified her eyes to almost comical proportions. "Hello, Capri, how are you?" Thelma's voice was warm, but she squinted, struggling to focus on Capri's face.

"Hey, Thelma." Capri slid her deposit bag across the counter. "You're gonna need to count this twice, Thelma. I wouldn't want your glasses playing tricks on you again."

"Now, don't you worry, I've got my eyes on these bills." Thelma chuckled, a good-natured sound, and started counting the money with exaggerated care.

Capri waited patiently, listening to the soft rustling of paper and the tick of an old clock on the wall, as Thelma painstakingly verified Capri's deposit, ensuring not a single dollar was amiss.

With receipt in hand, Capri thanked Thelma and turned for the door. Before she could reach for the handle, Nicola Cavendish appeared on the other side of the glass. She pushed open the door and immediately clamped onto Capri's elbow. "You were just the person I'd hoped to see this morning."

"Me? Why?"

"Have you heard?" A smug look blanketed the woman's features.

Capri dreaded asking. "Apparently not. What's up?"

Nicola shook her head in an exaggerated manner. "Doc Tillman is retiring. He and Winnie are packing up their house and moving to Florida to be near their son and his family."

"What?" Carol Deegan, who was sitting nearby at her desk, lifted from her chair and scurried over to join them. "Surely he's not closing down the clinic."

Capri's face broke into a smile. "No. I bet he's going to ask Lila to take over."

Nicola lifted her eyebrows. "That's the big news. He's handed over his practice to some guy from Texas. His name is Whit Calloway."

Capri's expression hardened. "Are you kidding me?"

Nicola swung her designer purse. "No. The clinic has a new owner."

Capri didn't bother to say another word. She turned and bolted out the door.

Minutes later she was at Reva's office door after ignoring Verna Billingsley's waving arms and warning that her boss was on the phone. Without bothering to knock, Capri pushed her way inside.

Reva looked up from her Zoom call, surprised.

Capri frantically motioned for her to hang up.

"Look, guys." She kept her eyes trained on Capri. "Something's come up. I need to go. I'll have Verna call you to reschedule." She pushed a button on her keyboard and the monitor went blank.

"This better be important," she told Capri.

"Get your purse," Capri demanded. "We're heading to Lila's. And if she's not there, we'll find her."

Worry crossed Reva's face. "Why? What's going on?"

Capri quickly filled her in. "I'll take my truck. You take your car. And call Charlie Grace."

Lila lived on the outskirts of town in a modest raw wood cabin nestled in pine trees. The covered front porch was adorned with two wicker chairs and pots of fading geraniums and sunflowers. A knit afghan was draped over the back of one of the chairs and an open book and an empty teacup rested on the nearby table.

Capri sprinted up the two steps and pounded on the door. Reva and Charlie Grace were both pulling in at the same time.

As they scrambled from their vehicles, Capri pounded again. She looked back at the girls and shook her head.

Reva stepped around her and pushed open the door. "Lila? Are you in there?"

"Her car's in the driveway," Charlie Grace reported. "She must be here."

Together they marched down the hallway to the door leading into their friend's bedroom. Reva lightly rapped. "Lila?"

"Go away," came a muffled answer.

The girls glanced between one another. Capri nodded and Reva turned the knob and gently pushed the door open.

They found Lila face down on the bed.

"Oh, honey," Reva said and immediately went to her side. She sat on the bed and patted her friend's back.

Capri parked her hands on her hips. "So, it's true then. Doc Tillman should be strung up and—"

Charlie Grace frowned at her. "Not helpful." She moved to the other side of the bed and sat next to her friend. "We're here for you, Lila."

Capri nearly growled. "I'll be back later."

Reva and Charlie Grace turned their attention her direction. "Where are you going?" Reva asked.

"To take care of some business."

Without waiting for either of them to interrogate her further, she charged out the door.

14

C apri pulled into the parking lot at the veterinary
clinic and rammed her Dodge D150 Adventurer into
park so fast, her tires spit gravel, not considering the
rocks might nick the bright red paint on her prized truck. Or
the shiny deep blue paint on the other pickup in the small
parking area—the only vehicle in sight.

Nonplussed, she scrambled from the driver's side and
slammed her door closed, then marched to the entrance.
Inside, she found the waiting room empty.

A sound coming from the back drew her past the check-in
counter and down the short hall that led to an examination
room. Before she could make her way fully to where the sound
was coming from, a guy stepped into the hallway.

He frowned. "Can I help you?"

"Where's Doc Tillman?" she demanded.

"Excuse me?" His frown deepened.

"Is he here?" Capri stepped around the guy and peered into
the exam room. Finding it empty, she glared back at the
stranger. "Where is he?"

She took a minute to assess the man before her. Clad in a

simple, well-fitted black T-shirt and rugged blue jeans that hinted at many days spent in nature, his casual attire did nothing to hide his lean, muscular frame.

"And you are?" he asked, his tone as dry as the desert.

"Capri Jacobs," she told him without breaking gaze. "Who are you?" The question answered itself. It didn't matter. She needed a name.

She paused and waited for him to meet her stare.

The guy almost grinned as he stroked his right ear lobe. "Whit Calloway. I'm the new vet here at the clinic. But something tells me you knew that."

She relented, but only slightly. "Yeah, small town. Word spreads fast."

He held out his hand to shake.

Reluctantly, she took his hand. She'd like to welcome him, but that would be disingenuous. "So, you're taking over here?"

Whit nodded. "That's the plan."

"The plan sucks," she said, not caring how her tart remark might be received.

He appeared to momentarily stiffen but recovered quickly. "So, I take it you're not happy with me being here?"

Capri leaned against the wall and folded her arms. "It's not you exactly. It's what you represent."

He shook his head. "Sorry, I'm not following."

She explained the situation. "One of my best friends, Lila Bellamy—well, she works here. Has for years."

This caused him to nod. "Ah..."

"Yes, and few know how many hours she's trained to become a veterinarian, with a large animal certificate. She always thought that if Doc Tillman decided to retire, he might offer the opportunity to buy this clinic and run it herself. So, understand when I tell you that you showing up on the scene isn't exactly welcome—not to her, and likely, not to this community." Her jaw set. "We take care of our own." Her tone was challenging and not at all welcoming. She knew some might judge her behavior as harsh and reprimand her for not being more friendly, but she didn't really care. Lila was heartbroken, and this guy was the reason why.

He rubbed at his lobe again. "Well, I hate hearing that. Really, I do. But you, and others here in town, can't really blame me. If Doc Tillman hadn't brought me on board, it would have been someone else. He told me he was anxious to move on with the next phase of his life after making the decision to retire. I'm not sure that he meant to hurt your friend."

Why didn't it surprise her that this new guy would take up for Doc and defend his decision? "Well, I guess you've never had your world ripped out from under you?" She glared at him. "And this isn't the first time." She explained Lila's history and how she'd lost her husband to an illogical war that had not only robbed her of the love of her life but her baby daughter's father. "She's a single mom who has faced more barriers to happiness than most, and each time she's climbed over the top of those walls and marched on, working hard and trying to find happiness." Capri tried to blink back tears. "So, you must understand how devastated she feels right now. This was her dream. Years of hard work, late nights, and juggling this job with motherhood. Then you appeared on the scene, and all that was for nothing."

To his credit, Whit's eyes softened. "I—yeah, I didn't know."

"Well, now you do." She straightened. "Question is, what are you going to do about it?"

15

"You did what?" Lightheaded from Capri's news, Lila dropped into a chair, unable to believe what she'd just been told. "What do you mean you talked to him?"

Capri shrugged as she slid into a chair opposite her at the kitchen table. "Yeah. I talked to him."

Reva carried the pot of coffee to the table. "Oh, Capri. I'm not sure that was a good idea."

Charlie Grace held up her mug to be filled. "Oh, I don't know. Maybe he needed to understand the situation. Clearly, Doc isn't broadcasting what little regard he has for all Lila's hard work."

Reva raised her eyebrows. "So, you don't find anything a little—uh, uncivil about confronting this guy? I mean, he was likely clueless in all this."

"Maybe," Capri admitted. "But that doesn't excuse the situation. The clinic should belong to Lila."

"You don't understand." Lila buried her head in her arms on the table and groaned. "He's the guy from the rodeo."

Capri glanced between the others, confused. "He's what?"

Lila straightened and reluctantly met their combined gaze. "My new boss is the same guy I confronted at the rodeo."

Charlie Grace let out a low whistle. "Well, that certainly complicates the situation."

Lila groaned. "What a mess."

Capri lifted a powdered donut from the plate on the table. "Mmm...my favorite kind." She stuffed her mouth and added, with her mouth full, "He needs you."

"Come again?" Lila asked.

Capri swallowed. "I said...he needs you. Think about it. Doc's record keeping was not stellar. You complained about it many times. The clinic's history is in your head, Lila. You know every person in town and their animals. You know what illnesses have been treated and who has paid and who hasn't."

Lila wasn't having any of it. "That doesn't matter. He can start fresh. He can learn."

"Maybe so," Reva said. "But it would be in his best interest to tap into one of his most beneficial resources...you."

Lila moaned. "I'll be lucky if he doesn't fire me. Not only did I get off on a bad foot, but my—" She jabbed a finger in Capri's direction. "My friend marched in and bit his head off. Yeah, I'm scoring points right and left."

She wrapped her hands around her coffee mug. "Thing is... I need this job. Camille is barreling toward high school graduation and all the expenses associated with that. Follow that up with getting my girl settled in college. All that on top of my regular expenses. And jobs aren't pinecones hanging on tree boughs around here. I can't simply pluck another—unless I want to flip burgers and schlep beer at Moosehead Tavern." She looked at them. "Veterinary medicine is my thing. I don't want to do anything else."

Charlie Grace reached across the table and took her hand.

"You don't have to quit, and he's not going to fire you. What you are going to have to do is figure out a way to work together." Her voice grew more firm. "You can do this, Lila," she said, her jaw set in determination.

Reva nodded enthusiastically. "This situation will all work out. You'll see."

Even Capri joined in. "Absolutely." She wiped her arm across her mouth to clear the remaining donut crumbs. "What they said."

The next morning, her friends' words rang in her head as she climbed from the shower and got ready. She rehearsed their encouragement again in the car as she drove to the clinic, mentally acknowledging that she'd grown accustomed to her dreams being elusive and unattainable, always just out of her reach. "I can do this," she said out loud as she unlocked the door and entered the clinic.

Lila flipped on the lights and went directly to the peg on the wall where she hung up her jacket. She tucked her purse in the cubby behind the front counter. Then she took out the clipboard and checked the appointments for the day.

The sound of an engine drew her attention to the front window. A sleek dark blue pickup pulled in and stopped, signally her new boss had arrived. Seconds later, the door opened, and he stepped inside. Upon seeing her, he cleared his throat. "Good morning, Lila."

"Morning," she forced a brightness she didn't feel.

"We need to talk," he said, rubbing at his right earlobe.

Oh, here it comes. He was going to fire her. And she wouldn't blame him. She'd been rude. He'd gotten into her business in that rodeo arena, and she hadn't held back in telling him so. Maybe not using those exact words, but her message had been clear.

She hadn't exactly been welcoming upon learning he was

taking over the clinic either. And only God Himself knew what Capri had said to him. Given the look on her face when she marched out of her house yesterday, Lila imagined her reprimand had been sharp as nails. What she couldn't imagine was how Whit Calloway had taken her harsh words.

Lila drew a deep breath. "Yeah, sure."

"Look, I think we got off on the wrong foot. I'd like to start over," he suggested.

Immediately relieved, Lila released the air she'd been holding. She still had a job at the clinic. At least for now.

She cleared her throat, willing her voice to be strong and firm. "Sure. We have a litter of pups coming in for vaccinations in about an hour, so we have a few minutes." She placed the clipboard on the counter. "Let's talk."

She trailed him to the back room.

"Uh, is there a coffee pot somewhere?" he asked.

She nodded. "Over here." She moved for a counter at the back of the room that held a sink with a line of cupboards above. At the far right, there was an older model Mr. Coffee machine, that frankly, had seen better days. "The filters and coffee grounds are in here." She opened a cupboard door and pulled out the items and proceeded to make coffee, adding an extra scoop. She needed her brew strong this morning. Liquid courage.

When she finished the task, she turned to find Whit leaning against the opposite counter, watching her. His gaze made her uncomfortable. She pointed her thumb back at the coffee maker. "Should be done soon."

He thanked her and invited her to follow him to the sofa against the left wall...a battered piece of furniture covered with animal hair. Normally, she would have brushed the seat before sitting. Not today. She simply sank into the cushion and watched as he took a place on the other end.

He opened his mouth, and she preempted him. "Look, I know Capri came to see you yesterday. She tends to be a little impulsive. Anything she said...well, she meant well. She's protective of the people she cares about."

Whit nodded. "Yeah, that girl's got some fire in her spirit. I admire her loyalty." He paused, gave her a long look. "I think I understand the situation now."

The comment got her dander up. He thought he understood? Not likely.

"Well, it's like this," she began. "Despite the fact I just made the coffee, that's not what I'm here to do. I have years of experience—general animal husbandry and veterinarian medicine. I've encountered a lot of precarious situations in my years here. I know my way around. I hope you don't think you have to coddle me, or—"

He laughed.

She stiffened. "Did you just laugh?"

Whit quickly put up his open palms. "I'm not laughing at you."

"Sounds like laughter to me. And we're the only ones in the room." For emphasis, she looked around. "No one but you and me."

He reached and pulled at his right earlobe. "Look, let me start over."

"Why do you always do that?"

"Do what?"

She pointed to his ear. "You pull on your ear."

His face flushed with color. "A nervous habit," he reluctantly admitted, his voice a bit defensive.

"Nervous?" Her eyebrows lifted. As soon as the words left her mouth, she could tell from his expression that he regretted his word choice.

It was then she began to consider his side of this situation. Maybe this wasn't all that easy on him, either.

He was taking on a whole new endeavor. While she wasn't privy to the financial end of things, no doubt he had an investment on the line. He was new to town. Despite being friendly, he would be sized up by the residents of Thunder Mountain in these early days. He'd have to earn their trust. Especially when dealing with their animals and precious pets.

Worse still, Nicola Cavendish would undoubtedly revel in broadcasting that Doc Tillman had favored the newcomer over her. Soon, everyone would be keeping their distance, blaming him just as she had.

Her demeanor softened slightly. Perhaps it was time to steer the conversation in a new direction. "Where are you from?" she inquired, tentatively aiming for a fresh start. "Let's start there."

Whit nodded. "I'm from Texas."

"I guess that explains the huge star emblem on your pickup." She fought to hold back an eye roll. "Must be a thing," she muttered.

Whit bristled. "Hey, there's nothing wrong with having pride in where you come from." His tone edged on the defensive. "That Lone Star? It's not just decoration—it's a symbol of pride. Not everyone gets it, I guess."

Lila shrugged, offering a half-hearted apology. "No offense meant. Everyone's got their thing, I suppose." Inside, she scoffed. Some people took things far too seriously.

Curious, despite her irritation, she asked, "What part of Texas?"

"Abilene," came his reply. Something came over his expression as he quickly added, "I grew up on a cattle ranch. Graduated from vet school and have been practicing for five years. I wanted to go out on my own when I heard of this opportunity through a posting on AVMA."

Lila immediately tensed. Doc posted the clinic was for sale through the American Veterinary Medicine Association? How could she not have known this? She often browsed the website.

"I knew this might be the very thing I was looking for, so I jumped on the opportunity."

Lila mentally calculated the timing. Had Doc posted the information recently—since his health episode? These things took time. There were attorneys and contracts and such. Did Doc have this in the works even before then?

She would probably never know unless she asked Doc directly, and she wasn't about to do that. Besides, he and Winnie were packing and would be pulling out of town soon. His mind was already on his new life...a life in Florida.

The thought both pleased her and made her extremely sad. Doc was the only boss she'd ever known. Despite his gruff nature, he had taught her a lot since the early days when she'd shown up and asked for a job, barely a widow and needing a way to support herself and her daughter.

He'd hired her as a front desk assistant, letting her progress over the years. His passion for animals fueled her own. He'd even encouraged her when she told him of her plans to enroll in school and get certified. Oh, he had his criticism, but she could tell he was pleased to hear she would become a vet.

Perhaps that is why his decision hurt so much.

Lila turned her attention back to Whit. "Did Doc tell you I would have my certificate soon?" Her tone carried a subtle challenge. She didn't want him discounting her contributions or abilities.

"He mentioned it," Whit told her. "I was glad to hear it, frankly. There can never be enough qualified hands on board. But we do need to come to an understanding."

"And that is?" She stared at his strong profile, his solid square face, high cheekbones, clean-shaven cheeks. Calloused hands.

He wasn't a city boy.

Whit shifted uncomfortably. "This clinic is under my direction. You're a valuable part of the team, and while I value your insights, the final calls are mine to make." He met her eyes, inviting her to challenge him.

There was a lot she wanted to say. Instead, she swallowed and pushed out an appropriate, and likely expected response. "Certainly," she said, her voice steady and cool. "This is your clinic."

16

L ila stuck her head inside the refrigerator, pulled out the last of the contents—a half-full mayonnaise jar and placed the glass container on the counter with the other items. After adjusting the red bandana on her head, which she wore to catch the few curls that always seemed to work their way loose, she dipped her rubber-gloved hand in the bucket of sudsy water and rung out the rag, then tackled wiping down the shelves with enough force to make the entire fridge shake.

She sighed and her thoughts drifted as she scrubbed at a particularly stubborn stain. It had been a long day at the clinic, and the last thing she wanted was to spend her evening cleaning out the refrigerator. But it needed to be done, and if there was one thing she had learned over the years, it was that chores didn't wait for anyone.

As she worked, her mind wandered to the clinic and the new owner, Whit Calloway. Just thinking about him made her grip the rag tighter. He had waltzed in with his Texan drawl and easy charm, turning her world upside down. Lila had always imagined herself taking over Doc Tillman's practice one day, not having to answer to someone else, especially not someone like Whit. Even so, she'd tried to be accommodating and helpful. But this new guy was nearly impossible to work with. Every day was a test of her patience as he tried to change everything.

The memory of their recent argument replayed in her mind —one of many they'd had in the past weeks. Whit had suggested reorganizing the clinic's back room. "I've ordered some bigger cabinets for the autoclaves and sterilization equipment, and a new cooler to store our vaccinations. Oh, and I have a new coffee maker on the way. The one we have is—" He made a face. "Ancient."

Lila had bristled at the implication that the way things were run in the clinic wasn't good enough. Even if it was true that their coffee maker was about to bite the dust.

She shook her head, trying to dispel the frustration that had settled in her chest. It wasn't just the changes; it was everything he represented—the upheaval of her plans, the challenge to her authority...and the unsettling way he made her heart race despite herself.

Whit Calloway was the kind of man who commanded attention without even trying, and that infuriated Lila more than she cared to admit. He was tall and broad-shouldered, with a rugged handsomeness that seemed to be chiseled by the Texan sun. His short-cropped brown hair framed a face marked by striking blue eyes that could be both disarmingly charming and infuriatingly cocky. The faint stubble on his jaw only added to his appeal, giving him a rough-edged allure that Lila found annoyingly attractive.

Despite her best efforts to focus on his infuriating tendencies—his unsolicited changes to the clinic, his casual confidence—she couldn't ignore the flutter in her stomach whenever he entered the room. A fact that only made her more determined to keep her guard up around him.

Lila stood, stretching her back, and glanced around the

kitchen. She caught sight of a photograph on the counter—a candid shot of her and her late husband, Aaron, taken on one of their many camping trips. She picked it up, tracing Aaron's smiling face with her finger. He had been her rock, her anchor, and losing him had left a void that nothing seemed to fill. She couldn't imagine what he'd have to say about all this.

Her thoughts were interrupted by the sound of the front door opening. Camille's cheerful voice called out, "Mom, I'm home!"

Lila smiled, setting the photo back down. "In the kitchen, sweetie!"

Camille bounded in, dropping her backpack on the floor, and peering into the empty refrigerator. "Something bothering you, Mom?"

Lila frowned. "What do you mean? I'm cleaning. This fridge hasn't been scrubbed in months."

Camille looked at her with patience. "I know. You always clean when you're upset."

"Oh?" Ignoring the accusation, she motioned her daughter over. "Maybe you can help."

Her daughter made a face. "I've got homework."

Lila parked her hands on her hips. "Well, if you want dinner on time, you'll need to help me finish this up. You can do homework after we eat."

Camille sighed. "I guess I can."

Lila chuckled. "That's the spirit." She handed Camille a rag and the two of them worked in companionable silence for a few minutes.

"Mom," Camille said after a while. "Do you like Dr. Calloway?"

Lila paused, caught off guard by the question. "Why do you ask?"

"I don't know. You just seem different when you talk about him. Like, more...intense."

Lila sighed, wiping her forehead with the back of her hand. "It's a bit complicated. But we're figuring it out."

Camille nodded, seeming to accept that answer. "Well, I think he's kind of nice. And he brought donuts to school for everyone when he did that talk about being a vet."

Lila grimaced. Now that Doc was retired, she'd hoped she would be the one invited to the school this year. Whit's arrival was ripping away her aspirations—as modest as they were. She'd had to adjust to the fact she wasn't taking over the clinic. The least he could do was move out of the way and let her in the spotlight for a moment.

"Everyone really liked what he had to say, Mom. He was so interesting. Some of the girls think he's cute."

Lila couldn't help but smile at that.

Camille dipped her rag in the bucket of warm, sudsy water, then wiped the top shelf. "I think he's nice."

"Yeah, he can be nice," Lila admitted.

Whit did have a way of winning people over. A parade of townspeople had made their way to the clinic over the past two weeks to meet the new veterinarian. The Knit Wits all brought casseroles and homemade canned goods. Nicola Cavendish brought her curiosity. Albie Barton carried a pad and paper with the intent to interview him for a feature in an upcoming issue of the *Thunder Mountain Gazette*.

Yes, everyone was pleased to have a new resident in Thunder Mountain.

Everyone but her.

17

Lila stared at the horizon, the jagged peaks of the Tetons cutting into the early evening sky. The rugged beauty of the landscape usually brought her a sense of calm, a rare respite from the chaos of her life.

Tonight, though, that calm eluded her as she traipsed out to the tiny makeshift barn Doc Tillman had erected over a decade ago. She carried a bucket of rabbit feed, taking dinner to the Jansen twins' two pet bunnies. They had parasites, and Whit wanted to keep them overnight so he could administer the necessary medicines.

Lila opened the cage. "You guys hungry?" She added clean straw to the cage, then filled the little feed troughs and gave them clean water. "Okay, there you go," she told the rabbits, smiling despite her mood as the bunnies gobbled down their pellets.

She heard the crunch of gravel under boots and turned to see Whit Calloway striding towards her, his expression unreadable.

Every time Whit looked at her, something inside Lila squirmed. He had a way of making her feel like he could see into the very depths of her soul with one glance like he knew all her secrets.

Thank goodness, her secrets were minimal and rather boring.

"Hey, I need you to go with me," he said, wrapping the hose and placing it back on the hook.

"Where?"

"Looks like a wolf may have got a wild horse up Lava Creek about halfway to Davis Hill."

"How bad?" While wolf attacks on horses were rare, it happened.

Whit motioned for her to follow as he turned and headed for the open sliding barn doors. "We'll know the full extent when we get there, but the BLM guy said it's leg looked pretty wicked."

She dropped the bucket near the base of the rabbit pen and made her way to the deep, plastic sink in the corner of the barn. She barely ran water over her hands and wiped them on her jeans as she scurried out of the barn.

Whit headed to the driver's side of his blue truck, climbed in, and hollered, "You coming?"

"Yes, I'm coming. Don't get your jeans in a twist." She stomped to the passenger side and threw open the door.

As soon as she climbed in, he shoved the gearshift into drive, and they took off.

She motioned out the rear window with her thumb. "You're taking the horse trailer?"

"We may need to transport the horse to a sanctuary in Lander. You know where that is?"

"Yeah. It's about a two-hour drive from Thunder Mountain." Lila glanced across the seat at him, then forced her gaze back to the road ahead.

"You ever load a skittish horse?" he asked.

She stared straight ahead. "Yep." She didn't tell him it was only once, and it was over five years ago.

Miles passed in silence as they made the drive southwest, stopping at an overlook so he could check the hitch.

While Lila took in the stunning panoramic view over the Teton Valley, Whit inspected the coupler and the safety chains, then dug into a cooler in the back of the pickup. "Want something to drink?" He held up a Dr Pepper.

"Yeah, thanks."

He climbed back into his truck and handed her an ice-cold can. She popped the tab, tipped the can up, and chugged the ice-cold drink like a pro.

They made it the rest of the way to Lava Creek in a little over a half hour, again riding in silence. At the junction to the dirt road bordering Lava Creek, she finally spoke up. "How far to where we need to pick up the horse?"

"Less than five miles," he answered.

She gazed out the window at the meandering banks of a stream, at crisscrossed pole fences winding through grassy meadows, and the pine-tree-covered mountains beyond.

In some ways, the craggy vista reminded her of the guy sitting inches away. He was most certainly a fine specimen, a man she found herself physically drawn to. He had a careless look, his jawline angular and rugged, even strong. But there was something in his eyes that told her Whit Calloway was not someone easily traversed, that he was studded with icy snow-capped spires extending too high to successfully climb.

Whit slowed the pickup and eased from the paved highway onto a rutted, potholed road that meandered through heavy sagebrush that scraped against the door of the truck. He looked across at her and apologized when he hit a particularly deep furrow.

She braced herself by holding onto the dash. "You ever work on a wild horse before?"

"A couple," he answered. Slowing, he maneuvered around the biggest of the dips, until they came to a wide-open space with nothing more than an empty corral and a small shed-like barn. A BLM vehicle was stationed nearby.

They parked and got out. As two BLM officials headed their way, Whit grabbed a lead rope from behind his seat.

"Hey, there!" one of the uniformed guys extended his hand. "You the vet? Glad you made it. That horse definitely needs medical attention."

Whit shut his pickup door and shook hands with both of the officers. "So, where is he?"

The tallest officer pulled his cap from his head and swiped his forearm across his brow. He nodded toward an old, dilapidated barn. "Horse is in there. Frankly, I'm surprised the wolf didn't do more damage."

The other officer stepped forward. "Here's the paperwork." He handed the envelope to Lila. She took the paperwork and tucked it inside the truck before following the three men to the barn.

At the door, the officers both hesitated. The one who had handed her the paperwork cleared his throat. "Well, that's all we need. Guess you can handle it from here."

Lila wanted to ask if he was kidding. Didn't they intend to help? A wounded horse was predictably hard to manage. It could very well take all of them to load the horse safely. She opened her mouth to say as much when Whit's hand went to her arm. "Thanks, guys. We've got it."

"Okay then, we'll be going."

She and Whit waited a few minutes for the men to get in their truck. As they were driving away, Lila turned. "What was all that? Don't you think those guys should have helped?"

"It's not help when it's not freely given." Whit had already turned, and his hand pulled the rusty handle on the door. The broken wooden panel creaked open. The entire structure looked like the rotted boards might collapse at any time.

Lila glanced back at the truck making its way in the distance, leaving a plume of dust trailing behind.

Inside, the barn was dusty and dark. At the last stall, Whit held up his arm, blocking her from going any farther. She paused behind him. The black mustang nearly got lost in the shadows except for his bared, yellowed teeth and the whites of his eyes. His ears lay flat back and he snorted, blowing snot and air.

"Whoa, boy." Whit slowly opened the stall door and took a cautious step forward. The young horse reared and lunged lopsided, striking out with his front hooves.

Her eyes widened. "I thought he was crippled."

Whit sidestepped easily and snapped the lead rope onto the halter as the horse's hoof banged into the side of the barn.

Lila threw open a wooden panel covering the window. "Maybe this will help."

In the light streaming from the opening, both she and Whit got a good look at the horse's injury—a gash that had nearly severed a tendon on his rear right leg. The wound was already infected.

Whit let out an expletive. "Looks like this horse suffered the attack a while ago."

Lila felt the start of tears and dashed them away before her new boss could see. She never got used to wounded horses, especially injuries of this magnitude.

After carefully looping a lead rope around the wild mustang's neck, Whit secured it tightly to the slats on the pen, ensuring the horse couldn't move too much. He knelt beside the wild mustang, his hands steady but gentle as he examined the nasty gash running along its leg. "This is pretty deep," he murmured, glancing up at Lila.

Her face was etched with concern, but her hands were

already moving with practiced efficiency, cleaning the wound with antiseptic. The mustang shivered, its eyes wide with fear and pain, but Lila's soothing voice and gentle touch seemed to calm it.

"We need to stitch this up," Whit said, reaching for the sutures. Lila nodded, her focus unwavering as they worked together, the tension between them momentarily forgotten in the shared goal of saving the injured animal.

Whit's broad shoulders and powerful arms hinted at years of hard work, yet there was a gentleness in the way he cradled the horse's leg, his fingers lightly caressing the length.

When he was finished stitching up the gash, Whit stroked the horse's velvety muzzle, but the young stallion yanked back from his touch, his eyes rolling wildly. "Best to get him loaded and out of here," he said to her. "I think I noticed a loading chute in the back. Might be safer to use that to get him loaded."

"I'll go get the trailer," she told him. Seeing the doubt in his eyes, she immediately turned defensive. "What? You don't think I can back a trailer?"

With only one try, she positioned the trailer at the chute with impressive precision. She climbed from the truck with great satisfaction and opened the back gate. "Your turn, cowboy."

Whit nodded with amusement. He slowly coaxed the horse forward, cueing him with a kissing sound. "Atta, boy. That's it." He gave the horse a gentle tap on the hind quarter with his open palm, urging the skittish animal toward the pile of hay placed at the front of the trailer as an incentive.

The process took time and several tries, but with Whit's carefully executed effort and softly spoken assurances, they got the job done. "Atta, boy. That's it." He fastened the safety bar and then the back gate.

He swiped his face with his bare forearm before moving to the ice chest in the back of his truck for a cold soda. He retrieved one for himself and tossed her one. "Well, that should do it."

Lila couldn't help but admire the way he'd handled the horse, with extraordinary patience and never showing anger. Animals sensed whom they could trust, and the young stallion responded accordingly.

She raised the can to her lips and took a large gulp—a careless gulp that left a bit of the soda escaping at the corner of her mouth.

Whit's gaze was relentless. His ability to maintain eye contact was something she had a hard time getting used to— the way he looked at her now with that blue stare as he removed his aviator sunglasses and tossed them on the dash.

"You need a napkin?" he asked.

She nodded.

As Whit leaned over to open the glove box, Lila's gaze drifted to the curve of his jaw, shadowed with a hint of stubble, and the way his short-cropped hair tapered at his neck—the way the muscles rippled in his back as he reached across her.

Her breath caught unexpectedly at the sight of his strong, capable hands moving with such assured precision. She hadn't felt this in years—a sudden, undeniable spark that sent warmth flooding through her. It startled her, this unexpected jolt of physical attraction.

She'd believed that part of her was forever dormant, but here she was, unable to ignore the flutter in her chest every time Whit's arm brushed against hers.

Her mind quickly drifted to what it would be like to kiss him.

The pit of her stomach warmed at the idea, and she chastised herself mentally.

He's your boss, she quickly reminded herself.

Whit looked at her again with one of those unreadable stares. "You good?"

She barely nodded. "Yeah.

"Well, let's get this injured horse to the sanctuary, shall we?"

The Wind River Wild Horse Sanctuary, located in Lander, Wyoming, was one of four public off-range equine refuges in the nation, and the only one located on an Indian reservation. The sanctuary included a visitor center that featured a curated, interpretive display describing the importance of the horse in the culture and traditions of Native Americans, as well as the history of wild horses in North America.

She'd visited while chaperoning a field trip for Camille's class.

On the way, she turned to Whit. "You think that leg's going to heal up?"

He beat his thumb against the steering wheel, clearly sharing her concern. "No doubt, that was a nasty gash. With some strong antibiotics and a little care, the horse should be good as new physically."

She dared another glance at the rolled-up sleeve on his arm that barely concealed his bulging bicep. "But?"

He slowly brushed his fingers across his stubbled chin and gave her another of those looks—this time staring intensely into her face. "No doubt pain can change an animal."

Suddenly, Lila didn't think they were talking about the horse anymore. "Are you implying something here? Because if you've got something to say, I invite you to just spit it."

Her new boss could have heard any number of things from the townspeople, especially Nicola Cavendish. She was a woman who could never be trusted.

"Nothing, it's just—"

"Just what?" she demanded.

His eyes softened. "Nothing."

"What did you hear?"

Whit didn't say anything for a few seconds. Finally, he cleared his throat and glanced over at Lila, his voice growing gentle. "I heard about your husband. I'm so sorry for your loss. It must've been tough, being alone all these years."

Lila's eyes flashed with a mix of surprise and indignation. "Alone? I haven't been alone. I've had my daughter, my friends, my work. Just because I haven't been in a relationship with a man doesn't mean my life hasn't been full."

Whit held up one of his hands in a placating gesture. "I didn't mean it like that, Lila. I just meant...it can't be easy. That's all."

Lila's posture relaxed slightly, but her voice remained firm. "I know you didn't. But I don't need anyone to feel sorry for me."

Whit's jaw stiffened and he gave a slight nod. "Understood."

The tension hung in the air, heavy and palpable, as the afternoon light began to fade. Lila turned her gaze out the truck window, watching rays of sunlight paint the distant mountains in hues of blue and purple. She took a deep breath, the beauty of the landscape offering a moment of solace.

They continued driving in silence, the truck rumbling down the dirt road toward the horse sanctuary. The quiet between them was thick, filled with unspoken words and lingering frustration. As they approached the sanctuary, the sight of the horses grazing peacefully in the pasture brought a brief sense of calm to Lila's mind.

"Look, I know you didn't mean any harm," she finally said, breaking the silence. "But my life is good. I don't need anyone thinking otherwise."

Whit nodded, his grip tightening on the steering wheel. "I get it. I really do."

As they pulled into the sanctuary, the truck came to a slow stop. Lila unbuckled her seat belt, her movements deliberate and firm. She turned to look at Whit, a mixture of frustration and confusion still swirling within her. There was something about him—an attraction that got under her skin in a way she hadn't felt in years. An appeal that had her unnerved.

"Well, here we are," Whit said quietly.

Lila's eyes drifted to the horizon. "Yeah, here we are."

They exited the truck together, the mountain air cool and still. As they walked toward the sanctuary gates, Lila couldn't shake the feeling that this unexpected partnership was going to be more complicated than she had ever anticipated.

18

A few days later, Lila pulled her car into an already packed parking area at Teton Trails Guest Ranch. "My goodness," she muttered, looking for a spot.

"There's a space," Camille called out, pointing.

"Thanks, baby." Lila eased her car into the tight spot between Pete and Annie Cumberland's pickup and Fleet Southcott's patrol car. "Careful when you get out," she warned her daughter. "We don't need any more dents in my car doors."

Reva was the one to suggest that Charlie Grace host an end-of-season barbecue, a celebration of the amazing success the new guest ranch had enjoyed the first year after opening. Charlie Grace was initially reluctant but quickly folded when she and Capri jumped on the idea during one of their Friday night get-togethers.

"Yes, you need a party!" Capri said. "Last spring, we were gifting you a new website. Now, look—you've had a season filled with guests."

"And your bank account shows it," Reva reminded. "Another season like this and you'll have your bank loan paid in full."

Capri nodded enthusiastically. "Everyone will want to help recognize all that you accomplished. Have the party," she urged. "Let's celebrate."

Charlie Grace could hardly argue with that.

Lila placed her arm around her daughter's shoulder as they headed for the crowd. From the looks of things, the entire town must be here.

Verna Billingsley was standing by the firepit chatting with the Knit Wits, each one dressed to the hilt. Oma Griffith had on a bright orange pair of pants with a tropical print shirt. Betty Dunning's outfit was a bit more sedate—jeans and a white button-down top. She did have on a pair of bright red flats that matched the bracelets on her wrist. Dorothy Vaughn chose a flowing skirt in a western motif and cowboy boots. The gals were all cute as buttons.

Charlie Grace's dad, Clancy, was in his wheelchair near the barbecue pit, talking animatedly and pointing to the steaks on the grill. Based on the look on Ford Keaton's face, he didn't appreciate the cooking advice.

Albie sat in a lawn chair near a big pine tree. He wore a wide smile as he jiggled his niece's chubby baby on his lap while Lizzy took the moment of freedom and headed for the beer keg to join her husband, Gibbs.

Wooster and Nicola Cavendish were there. As was Diane Robinson and her young daughter. Seems everyone was taking the opportunity to celebrate and enjoy the beautiful evening.

Lila took a deep breath, feeling a sense of belonging as she looked around. She squeezed Camille's shoulder and smiled. "Let's go find Capri and the others," she said, leading her daughter into the heart of the gathering.

They wove through the clusters of people, greeting familiar faces along the way. Lila spotted Capri near the gazebo, deep in conversation with Reva and Charlie Grace. She gave Camille a gentle nudge toward the refreshment table. "Why don't you grab us some lemonade, sweetie?"

Camille nodded and headed off, leaving Lila to join her friends. "Looks like the whole town showed up," she said, moving into the circle.

"Of course, they did," Capri beamed. "No one wants to miss Charlie Grace's parties."

Charlie Grace chuckled, her eyes scanning the crowd. "I think it's more about the company and the yummy food than the party planning."

Reva nudged Lila playfully. "Speaking of company, guess who just arrived?"

Lila followed Reva's gaze and her heart sank. Whit Calloway. He stood near the edge of the gathering, looking somewhat out of place in his polished boots.

Lila's stomach tightened. "Great," she muttered. "Just what I needed."

"Maybe he's not so bad," Capri suggested, her eyes twinkling mischievously. "Why don't you go say hello?"

"Not a chance," Lila replied quickly, shaking her head. "I'm not in the mood for another run-in."

"Why? Did something else happen?" Charlie Grace asked.

Sure, she could explain how he'd accused her of having no life, but her friends would likely take his side. She wasn't up to arguing her point—not with them or with her new boss.

To her relief, Whit approached Pastor Pete and Annie. Whatever he said made Annie laugh. She continued to watch as he finished his conversation and headed for the barbecue pit, where large burlap-wrapped beef roasts had been slow-cooking for hours. He surveyed the setup and chatted with Ford, the cook. Ford led him to the grills where steaks were cooking.

Whit was dressed in a well-worn black T-shirt that hugged his athletic frame and a pair of faded jeans that fit just right.

The baseball cap on his head bore some sort of logo and his eyes were hidden behind aviator sunglasses. A loyal hunting dog with a sleek coat and expressive eyes trailed beside him, the bond between man and animal evident in every shared glance and easy smile.

"Lila. Did you hear me?" asked Reva.

Her attention snapped back to the group. "Oh, I'm sorry. What did you say?"

Reva pushed her sunglasses up on her head. "I asked how things were going at the vet clinic with Doc Tillman gone."

Lila sighed. "Fine." Her answer was short and clipped. She didn't want to admit the tension that pervaded, or how often Whit had new ideas and methods that irked her. That would make her sound petty.

The truth was, Whit had gone out of his way to include her on what he termed "the team." He never hesitated to ask her along when the wild horse got hurt and needed treatment and then a transport to the sanctuary. He asked her opinion and didn't hover over her every move like Doc Tillman often had. To anyone on the outside, she had little reason to feel negative toward her new boss.

Yet, she did.

Before the conversation could continue, Ford rang the metal triangle, sending out a loud clanging sound that called everyone to dinner.

"Oh, good. I'm starving," Capri said, heading that way.

The aroma of sizzling steaks wafted through the crisp mountain air, mingling with the delicious scent of roast beef slowly cooking in a buried pit nearby. The grill crackled and hissed, each pop releasing a burst of smoky fragrance that promised a feast to remember. Tables groaned under the weight of homemade sides: creamy coleslaw, tangy baked beans, buttery cornbread, and crisp garden salads topped with fresh vegetables. The scent of barbecued ribs, smothered in a tangy sauce, mingled with the sweet smell of corn on the cob, roasted to perfection.

As partygoers lined up with plates in hand, conversations floated on the breeze—neighbors catching up, friends sharing laughter, and children's excited chatter. The clink of utensils and the clatter of plates blended with laughter and the sound of crickets chirping rhythmically from the grassy edges of the clearing.

Lila caught sight of Reva's loyal assistant, Verna Billingsley. She waved, and Verna waved back.

"Hey, Verna. How's it going?" Lila asked.

The older woman shook her head. "Well, the office rebuild project finally got finished. It liked to have been months working in all that dishevel."

"Reva said you were a real trooper. That you kept right on top of the construction effort and everything that entailed," she said, hoping the compliment might erase the sour look on the woman's face.

Verna harrumphed. "Somebody had to. Jumping through government hoops is a real trial...know what I mean?"

Lila suppressed a laugh. In this case, the government was Reva and a town council that rarely crossed her. She doubted the project had been held up with red tape.

As the sun began to dip behind the majestic Teton Mountains, casting a warm golden glow over the gathering, the sounds of contented chatter started to fade. Plates were emptied, and satisfied sighs could be heard as guests leaned back in their chairs, savoring the last bites of their hearty meal.

The aroma of grilled meat still lingered in the air, but now it was joined by the soft strumming of a guitar. The band, positioned under a rustic wooden pavilion, began to tune their instruments, drawing curious glances and eager smiles from the crowd.

Slowly, the hum of conversation quieted, replaced by the

anticipatory hush that always precedes the first note of live music. With a final, harmonious chord, the band signaled the start of the evening's entertainment, and the guests began to shift their attention, ready to enjoy the next phase of the celebration.

Nick Thatcher took Charlie Grace by the hand. "I think that's our cue to dance."

She smiled back at her boyfriend before following him out to the floor. As they swirled to the music, the crowd applauded and cheered.

"You go, Charlie Grace!" called someone from the crowd.

Kellen found his way to Reva, Lucan in his arms. "Will you do me the pleasure, Mrs. Warner?" She granted him a wide smile. "I thought you'd never ask." The three of them moved to the dance floor where they began swaying to the music.

Capri spotted her mom and stepdad across the way. She scrambled over and grabbed the handles of his wheelchair. "Sorry, Mom. This dance is mine." Her eyes twinkled as she wheeled her cancer-ridden stepfather onto the makeshift dance floor and whirled him around the wooden deck to the tune.

When the song ended, Dick reached for Capri's hand. He patted it with an appreciative look on his face. Even from a distance, Lila could see him mouth the words, "Love you, sweetheart."

Lila's eyes were drawn back to Whit, who seemed to be scanning the area, looking for someone. Before she could turn away, he caught sight of her and started heading in her direction.

"Oh no," Lila whispered to herself, trying to edge away, but it was too late. Whit reached her side, his blue eyes twinkling with a mischievous glint.

"Evening, Lila," he said smoothly. "Enjoying the party?"

"Trying to," she replied, her voice curt.

Whit didn't seem fazed. "Well, let's say we make it even better. Would you care to dance?" He extended his hand, and Lila stared at it for a moment, her mind racing.

Dancing with Whit was the last thing she wanted to do. But before she could form a proper excuse, her feet betrayed her, stepping forward. She took his hand. The warmth of his grip sent a jolt through her, and she felt an unexpected flutter in her chest.

As they moved to the makeshift dance floor, Lila was acutely aware of the curious stares following them. Whit's hand settled at her waist, pulling her slightly closer, and she had to remind herself to breathe. The music swirled around them, and despite her initial resistance, she found herself relaxing slightly.

"You look really nice tonight," Whit said softly, his voice barely audible over the music.

Lila's heart skipped a beat. "Thanks," she managed to say, feeling a blush creep up her neck. She glanced up at him, and for a moment, she saw past the polished exterior to the man underneath. His eyes held a sincerity that took her by surprise, and she realized once again that Whit Calloway was undeniably attractive.

As Lila swayed in Whit's arms, she felt a warmth spread through her. His hand resting gently on her lower back sent shivers up her spine, and the steady rhythm of his heartbeat against her cheek was oddly comforting. Every step they took together felt like a silent conversation, a promise of something unspoken yet deeply understood.

The song ended too soon, and as they stepped apart, Lila felt a strange mix of relief and disappointment. Whit gave her a smile that did funny things to her stomach. "Thank you for the dance," he said.

Lila nodded, struggling to find her voice. "You're welcome."

As Whit walked away, Lila stood there, her mind spinning.

Maybe Capri was right—perhaps Whit Calloway wasn't so bad after all.

The evening's festivities continued in full swing when a hush fell over the crowd, followed by murmurs of excitement. Lila turned to see the source of the commotion and spotted none other than Roxie Steele, the visiting enigmatic and glamorous romance author making her grand entrance. Draped in a figure-hugging red dress that shimmered under the string lights, Roxie exuded confidence and charm. Her arrival was like a bolt of lightning, electrifying the atmosphere.

Aware of the attention, Roxie sauntered through the gathering with an easy grace, her eyes sparkling with mischief. She made a beeline for the group of older men gathered near the firepit, her laugh carrying over the music like a seductive melody.

Clancy Rivers was the first to fall under her spell, his cheeks flushing as she leaned in close, whispering something that made him chuckle and adjust his hat. She moved on to Ford Keaton, trailing a perfectly manicured hand along his arm, eliciting a bashful smile from the usually stoic rancher. Even Albie, holding his niece, blushed profusely as Roxie winked and blew him a kiss.

Roxie's playful flirting left a trail of blushing faces and stammered compliments in her wake. The older men, normally reserved, competed for her attention, their grins wide and their spirits high. Watching the scene unfold, Lila exchanged amused glances with her friends, their laughter ringing out into the night air.

Lila glanced up to find Whit standing next to her, a grin on his face. "Who's that?" he asked.

"That's Roxie Steele." She explained how the visiting romance author had captured the town's attention, especially the older male residents.

He shook his head and let out a low whistle. "I can see that."

The party began to wind down, and Roxie, with a final dazzling smile and a twinkle in her eye, sauntered back to her cabin. As she disappeared into the night, Whit turned to Lila and said with a grin, "Well, I guess there's no arguing that romance is well and alive, even in the wilds of Wyoming."

Lila chuckled, feeling the warmth of his gaze on her. "Seems like it," she replied, her heart jumping a beat. The soft glow of the stringed lights cast shadows that highlighted the sharp angles of his face.

For a moment, they stood there, the sounds of the party fading into the background. Whit's eyes softened as he took a step closer. "You know, Lila," he said, his voice low and inviting, "I had a really good time tonight. I think I'm going to like it here."

Lila's breath caught as their eyes locked, a spark of tentative truce igniting between them. She froze with the astonishing revelation that her feelings for Whit were betraying her, evolving into something she couldn't quite name. Even if he annoyed the pete out of her, she was attracted to him.

She supposed it wouldn't hurt to at least give the Texan a chance. Besides, what choice did she have really? Whit Calloway was here to stay. She might as well drop her rocks and get on with it. It might work in her favor if they at least became friends.

The music slowed to a gentle, romantic tune, and Whit extended his hand once more. "Care for another dance?"

Lila hesitated for several heartbeats before taking his hand, her pulse quickening. "Sure. I'd like that."

The stars shimmered like diamonds against the velvety black sky as Whit and Lila found their way onto the makeshift dance floor. Hesitant at first, Lila allowed Whit to draw her into the dance. His strong arms encircled her waist, pulling her closer than she had anticipated. She again became acutely aware of his presence—the solidness of his build, the warmth radiating from his body, and the intoxicating blend of cedar and leather that clung to him. It was a scent so uniquely male that it stirred something deep within her.

As they swayed to the music, a deep longing bloomed within her. Her heart quickened, and she found herself leaning into Whit's touch, savoring the feeling of being held.

But just as her guard began to fall, an image of Aaron formed in her mind. His familiar smile, the feel of his embrace, the life they had built together—it all came rushing back. She felt as if she were betraying him, her love for him. It didn't make sense, but guilt gnawed at her.

Panicked, Lila abruptly pulled away, mumbling an incoherent excuse about needing air. Without waiting for Whit's response, she fled into the night, her heart a tumble of longing and sorrow.

Capri grabbed her by the elbow as she passed by. "Hey, what was that about? Are you okay?"

Lila stopped, her breath coming in ragged gasps. "I...I don't know, Capri. I just couldn't—"

Capri's eyes softened with understanding. "Is this about Aaron?"

A tear slid down Lila's cheek as she nodded. "I felt like I was betraying him. I haven't felt this way in so long, and it scared me." She groaned and dared to glance back at Whit who stood on the dance floor watching her. "It's been years, but somehow it felt like Aaron was right next to me on that dance floor."

Capri pulled her into a comforting hug. "It's okay to have romantic feelings again, Lila. Aaron would want you to be happy, to move on with your life. It doesn't mean you're forgetting him or what you had together."

Lila sniffed, resting her head on Capri's shoulder. "I know, but it's so hard. I didn't expect to feel anything like that again, and now it's all so confusing."

Capri squeezed her tighter. "Take your time. Nobody is expecting you to have it all figured out right now. Just know that it's okay to let yourself feel again, to open up to new possibilities." She cupped Lila's face in her hands. "Whit Calloway is a hunk. Even if he is your boss."

Lila pulled back, letting herself laugh. She wiped her tears. "Thanks, Capri. You're right. He is."

"Anytime," Capri said with a reassuring smile. "Now, let's get you home. You've had enough excitement for one night."

As they walked away from the party with Camille following close behind, Lila couldn't help but glance back at Whit, who stood watching her with a mix of concern and something deeper.

"He must think I'm an idiot," she muttered under her breath. "Running off the dance floor like that."

Capri squeezed her hand. "You're an idiot if you close yourself off to someone who's so clearly interested. Did you see the way he looked at you?"

Camille laughed. "Yeah, Mom. Capri's right. I think he's really into you."

Lila nodded, then took a deep breath, knowing she had a lot to sort out. But for the first time in a long time, she felt a flicker of possibility.

19

Lila stood at her kitchen counter, arranging an assortment of snacks and drinks on a large wooden tray. The familiar sound of laughter and chatter filled her small mountain home as Charlie Grace, Reva, and Capri settled into the living room. It was their tradition to gather on Friday nights, a ritual that provided a comforting anchor amid their busy lives. But this week, their get-together had been moved to Sunday night to accommodate the barbecue out at Teton Trails.

"Do you need some help?" called out Reva.

"Nope. I got it." Lila scooped up the tray and headed to join them.

"I can't believe how big Lucan is getting," remarked Charlie Grace as she reached for a stuffed mushroom.

Reva nodded. "I know, right? The other day he decided he wanted to pour his own milk. Before I could stop him, he had the milk carton poised over his cup and was filling it up. Unfortunately, he didn't stop, and milk went everywhere. It was like watching a slow-motion disaster." She laughed, shaking her head. "By the time I managed to grab the carton from him, there was a puddle spreading across the table and dripping onto the floor. The look on his face was priceless though—and so proud of himself."

Charlie Grace chuckled, leaning back on the couch. "Kids have a knack for making the simplest tasks into epic adventures, don't they?"

Capri smiled, taking a sip of her wine. "Speaking of adventures, how's everything with the new vet?"

Lila couldn't help but feel her shoulders tense at the mention of his name.

Capri slipped a slice of cheddar from the tray. "Oh, I see that look on your face. You need to get over your reservations. Whit Calloway is a catch."

Charlie Grace sighed. "Agreed. If I wasn't already taken, I'd have to give you a run for your money. I mean, they grow them good in Texas."

Lila raised her eyebrows and turned to Capri. "You told them?"

"Of course, I told them. "

Reva unscrewed the top off her bottle of sparkling water. "We have no secrets. You know that."

Charlie Grace placed her hand on Lila's knee. "I suppose it's normal for you to feel you are betraying Aaron, but honey— he'd want you happy. You know that, right?"

Capri leaned back into the sofa cushions. "Camille was a baby. She's nearing high school graduation. That's a long time, Lila."

"Okay, I get that. But it's complicated."

Reva filled her glass. "Speaking of Camille, what does she think of your new boss?"

Lila sighed, brushing a stray hair from her face. "She's curious about him, I guess. I mean, she's always asking questions. Wants to know if he's as strict as Doc Tillman or if he's nice. The other day, she even urged me to have him over for dinner."

Reva lifted her glass. "What did you say?"

Lila ran a hand over the side of her hair. "I told her I didn't think that was a good idea. At least not right now."

Charlie Grace laughed softly. "She's got the right idea. It appears she senses something you're not ready to admit."

Lila groaned, leaning her head back against the couch. "Can we not make this into a big thing? It's already stressful enough trying to keep things professional at the clinic."

Capri tilted her head, her eyes softening. "We're not trying to pressure you, Lila. We just want you to be open to possibilities. Whit or no Whit, it's about you giving yourself a chance to be happy again. Besides, I read somewhere that lady parts can atrophy over time, if not used."

"Capri!" Reva scolded.

Their naughty friend grinned. "No, really...I read it."

Lila's gaze drifted to the window, where pine trees were silhouetted with a twilight sky painted in hues of pink and orange. "I appreciate the concern, really. It's just...this situation is a bit tangled. But I'll think about what you've all said, okay?"

Reva raised her glass in a mock toast. "That's all we ask. To possibilities and finding joy where we least expect it."

Lila clinked her glass with Reva's, a small smile playing on her lips. "To possibilities."

20

F ive days later, that possibility seemed more real than ever. Lila stood in the clinic's break room, nervously adjusting her scrubs as she prepared for another day under Whit Calloway's watchful eye. She had tried to push the conversation with her friends to the back of her mind, but their words echoed in her thoughts.

Whit walked in, his usual confident stride making her heart skip a beat. "Morning, Lila," he said with a warm smile. "Ready for another busy day?"

Lila nodded, trying to match his enthusiasm. "Always."

As they worked side by side, she couldn't help but notice the small, thoughtful gestures Whit made—how he ensured she had the tools she needed, the way he patiently explained complex cases, and the genuine care he showed for their animal patients and their owners.

It was becoming harder to ignore that her original assessment had been wrong. She was getting to like him—far more than she had expected.

Once, Whit had reached from behind her to pull a box of

syringes off the shelf. His breath on her cheek made her blush. And a tingle ran down her spine.

She hadn't tingled over a man for a very long time.

She'd spent more than one sleepless night thinking about it all. So many questions swirled in her mind in the dark.

She didn't know Whit's middle name or what size shoes he wore...or what made him laugh until he cried. She tried to picture what his hair looked like first thing in the morning when it was messy. What was his preference in take-out food? What were his dreams he never said out loud but secretly wished to come true?

Lila felt like a schoolgirl, thinking about Whit all the time.

She knew she had to be cautious, though. Her heart had been dormant for a long time and the fear of opening up again was almost paralyzing. But something about Whit made her want to take that risk, to trust again. Maybe it was the way he genuinely cared for the animals or the way he always seemed to know when she needed a moment of silence or a kind word.

Or the way he looked at her when he brought her a mug of coffee in the morning.

Was it possible he felt the same attraction for her?

It seemed so, but there was no way to know for sure. Not unless she came out and asked him. She'd rather die than be that vulnerable. What could he possibly say if she'd assumed his feelings were more than they were? He might have been simply being kind and thoughtful.

Whit came up behind her and looked over her shoulder at the clipboard she held. "What have we got up for this morning?" he asked, standing so close she could smell his cologne.

"Uh, Fleet Southcott's Lab had a litter of pups. He found homes for all but one. We're spaying the little female he decided to keep."

As if on cue, the front door opened.

Whit smiled warmly at Fleet as he entered the clinic. "Good morning, Fleet. How's our little patient doing today?"

Fleet gave a nervous chuckle, glancing down at the sleeping puppy in his arms. "Morning, Dr. Whit. This is Nala. And she's good. Honestly, I think I'm more worried than she is."

Lila stepped forward, reaching out to gently stroke the pup's head. "It's completely normal to feel that way, Fleet. She's in good hands, though. We'll take excellent care of her."

Whit nodded in agreement. "Absolutely. This is a routine procedure, and we'll make sure she's comfortable and well taken care of throughout the procedure."

Fleet took a deep breath, his grip on the pup tightening slightly. "I know, I know. It's just...she's quickly become part of the family, you know? I want to make sure she's okay."

Whit placed a reassuring hand on Fleet's shoulder. "I get it. I really do. We understand how much she means to you. We'll keep you updated every step of the way. Should take less than an hour and you'll have her back before you know it."

Fleet's tension seemed to ease a bit at Whit's words. "Thanks, Dr. Whit. That means a lot."

Whit turned to Lila. "Why don't you take Fleet and his pup into the exam room, and I'll prep the operating room? We'll get started soon."

Lila nodded, smiling at Fleet. "Come on, let's get her settled in. We'll take good care of her, I promise."

As they moved toward the exam room, Lila couldn't help but notice how Whit's presence seemed to calm both her and Fleet. His confidence and kindness were qualities she admired more and more each day. It made her wonder what other facets of him she had yet to discover.

Once they were in the exam room, Lila helped Fleet place the puppy on the table. She gently stroked the pup's fur, speaking softly to reassure both the animal and its owner. "She'll be just fine, Fleet."

Fleet nodded, giving the pup one last affectionate pat before stepping back. He stroked his handlebar mustache. "I know she will. Thanks, Lila."

Whit entered the room a few minutes later, fully prepped and ready. "Alright, let's get started. Fleet, you can wait out front. I think we have some recent copies of Horseman magazine. We'll come get you as soon as we're done."

Fleet hesitated for a moment, then nodded. "Okay. I'll be right outside."

As Fleet left the room, Whit turned to Lila. "Ready?"

Lila took a deep breath. "Ready."

Whit smiled, and for a moment, their eyes met, sharing an unspoken understanding and connection. Then, with a nod, they turned their attention to the task at hand, working together seamlessly to care for the little pup.

The spay procedure went as expected and soon, little Nala and Fleet were reunited.

Fleet drew her into his arms. "I can't thank you enough, you two."

Lila handed him a sheet of printed instructions. "Here's what you need to know for taking care of Nala over the next few days."

Fleet took the paper and listened attentively as Lila explained. "For the next ten to fourteen days, you need to keep her as calm and quiet as possible. No running, jumping, or rough play. Leash walks only."

Whit joined them wiping his hands with a towel. "Check her incision site daily for any signs of swelling, redness, or discharge. It's normal to see a bit of redness, but if it looks very inflamed or if there's any oozing, give us a call immediately."

Fleet nodded that he understood. "And this?" He pointed to the soft cone around the pup's neck.

Lila straightened the device. "Make sure she doesn't lick or chew at her stitches. We've given her this soft cone to wear, and she should keep it on until the stitches are removed in about a week."

Whit smiled reassuringly. "She's a strong little pup, and she should recover quickly. But if you have any questions or concerns, we're here for you."

Fleet nodded, looking relieved. "Thanks, both of you. I really appreciate it."

"No problem at all," she said. "We'll check in with you in a couple of days to see how she's doing. Take care, Fleet."

As Fleet carried Nala out of the clinic, Lila felt a warm sense of accomplishment. She loved helping animals and their owners, and moments like this made her feel grateful for her work, and maybe a bit closer to Whit, too.

Lila hated to admit it, but working with Whit wasn't so bad, after all. Unlike Doc Tillman, Whit seemed to respect her knowledge and ability. She was never made to feel inferior and was considered an important part of the veterinary team.

As the day wound down and they finished up the last of their appointments, Lila found herself lingering in the break room, her thoughts racing. She couldn't shake the growing attraction she felt towards Whit, nor the warmth that seemed to blossom whenever they worked together. She knew she had to do something about it, but the idea of making the first move filled her with nervous energy.

Whit entered the room, his easy smile making her heart skip a beat. "Hey, Lila. You did a great job today. Thanks for handling everything so smoothly."

Lila smiled back, trying to gather her courage. "Thanks, Whit. It's been good working with you."

There was a moment of silence, the kind that could stretch awkwardly if left unattended. Lila took a deep breath, deciding it was now or never. "Whit, I was thinking...my daughter will be out with friends tonight. I hate eating alone. If you're not busy, maybe you'd like to come over for dinner? Just a casual meal. I owe you for all the help you've been giving me here."

Whit raised an eyebrow, a hint of surprise in his eyes, followed by a genuine smile. "Dinner? That sounds great, Lila. I'd love to."

Lila's heart raced. "Really? Great! I mean, good. I'll, uh, cook something nice."

Whit chuckled softly. "I'm sure whatever you make will be fantastic. What time should I come over?"

"How about seven?" she suggested, her nerves slightly easing with his enthusiasm.

"Seven it is," Whit agreed. "Need me to bring anything?"

"Just yourself," Lila said with a smile. "I'll take care of the rest."

As Whit left to finish up his paperwork, Lila felt a mix of excitement and anxiety. She couldn't believe she had actually invited him over. The rest of the day passed in a blur as she finished her tasks and made her way home to prepare.

By the time seven o'clock rolled around, Lila had set the table and cooked a simple yet delicious meal of roasted chicken with vegetables, a fresh salad, and a homemade apple pie for dessert. She was just lighting a couple of candles on the table when the doorbell rang.

Taking a deep breath to steady herself, Lila opened the door to find Whit standing there, holding a bottle of wine, and wearing a warm smile. "Hey, Lila. This is for you," he said, handing her the wine.

"Thanks, Whit. Come on in," Lila replied, stepping aside to let him enter.

As they settled around the table to eat, the conversation flowed easily, moving from their shared experiences at the clinic to their lives outside of work.

After dinner, Lila invited Whit into the living room. "Would you like more wine? I have a bottle of pinot noir from a winery in Oregon you might enjoy."

"Sure, I'd like that."

She grabbed the bottle and a corkscrew from her wine rack. They moved to the sofa.

"Here, let me," Whit offered. He uncorked the bottle and poured, filling their glasses.

As they sipped on their wine, the conversation turned deeper, more personal. She told him about her classes and how excited she was to finish and get her certification.

"Did you always know you wanted to work in this field?" he asked.

Lila chuckled and shook her head. "No, I stumbled into it. After Aaron died, I needed a job. Doc Tillman needed an assistant. I had no experience, but he took pity and offered to train me." She kicked off her shoes and tucked her feet up under her on the sofa. "What about you?"

Whit leaned back on the couch, his eyes reflecting the warm candlelight. "Like you, I wasn't always planning on being a vet. My dad wanted me to join the family ranching business, but I quickly realized my heart wasn't in it." He paused, seeming to reflect on what he was about to say. "That didn't exactly set very well."

Lila stared at him wide-eyed. "I'm so sorry. Have you smoothed things over?"

Whit shook his head. "Not entirely. My mother quickly joined my dad's side when I announced I was moving to Wyoming. I mean, she was fine with me following my aspirations, so long as I practiced in Texas...preferably within twenty miles of Abilene." He laughed lightly before adding, "The sprawling cattle ranch I grew up on was originally in my mother's family. She was firm in her expectation that the next generation step up and take over. Since I am an only child, that landed on me."

"Wow, that's a lot," Lila said, filling his wine glass.

"Yeah, the whole family legacy thing. It can be heavy, you know?"

After completing his veterinary studies and gaining several years of experience, Whit's desire for a fresh start and to escape the weight of his family's expectations led him to move to the Tetons after seeing the notice that Doc Tillman's practice was up for sale. "The scenic beauty and tight-knit community offered me the perfect opportunity to redefine my identity and start anew, far from the shadow of my family ranch...and other accompanying complications."

Lila looked at him, intrigued. "What made you switch to veterinary medicine?"

Whit smiled softly, a distant look in his eyes. "There was this stray dog that used to hang around the ranch. I started feeding him, and one day he got hit by a car. I rushed him to the nearest vet, and the way they saved his life...it just clicked for me. I knew that's what I wanted to do—help animals. So, I switched majors, and here I am."

Lila nodded, feeling a new depth of understanding and admiration for Whit. "That's incredible, Whit. I had no idea. It's amazing how life can change direction like that."

Whit chuckled. "Yeah, it is. And coming here, to this town, meeting you...it's one of the best changes I've made."

Lila's heart skipped a beat. Meeting her had fed the equation that added up to his satisfaction with the move.

Lila found herself relaxing, enjoying Whit's company and the way he made her laugh.

Whit turned to her, his expression thoughtful. "You know, Lila, I've really enjoyed getting to know you. I wasn't sure what to expect when I came here—especially after that first meeting at the rodeo—but you've helped make Thunder Mountain feel like home."

Lila felt a warmth spread through her chest at his words.

"I'm glad you feel that way. I've enjoyed getting to know you, too. More than I expected."

There was a moment of silence, filled with unspoken possibilities. Whit reached out and gently took her hand. "I know this might be sudden, but I think there's something special between us. I'd like to see where it goes if you're willing." He cleared his throat. "I know I'm technically your boss, but I hope that won't be a problem. I feel like we're a team, you know?"

Lila's heart raced, but she felt a sense of certainty she hadn't felt in a long time. "I'd like that too, Whit."

As they sat there, hand in hand, Lila realized that maybe, just maybe, she was ready to open her heart again. Yes, things were complex, but the complications were worth working out.

The idea of Whit by her side felt like the start of something truly beautiful.

Whit turned to her, his gaze soft and intense. He gently cupped her cheek, leaning in slowly. Lila's breath hitched, her heart pounding as he closed the distance between them. Just as their lips were about to meet, the front door burst open, and a chorus of giggles filled the room.

"Mom, we're home!" Camille's voice rang out, followed by the sound of several teenage girls chattering excitedly.

Lila and Whit quickly pulled apart, both of them flustered.

Camille entered the living room with her friends, her eyes widening when she saw Whit sitting so close to her mother. "Oh! Hi, Dr. Calloway. I forgot you were coming for dinner."

Whit cleared his throat, standing up and giving Lila a sheepish smile. "Hey, Camille. We were just...catching up after work."

Camille glanced between them, a knowing look in her eyes. "Right. Well, these are my friends, Ashley, Brooke, and Jenna. We're just going to hang out in my room for a bit."

The girls waved and smiled, trying to stifle their giggles as they followed Camille down the hall.

Lila could feel her face burning with embarrassment. "Sorry about that," she said, trying to laugh it off.

Whit chuckled, running a hand through his hair. "No need to apologize. They're great kids."

Lila sighed, feeling both relief and disappointment at the interruption. "Yeah, they are. Maybe we can pick this up another time?"

Whit nodded, his eyes still holding that same warmth and affection. "I'd like that. Very much."

As he gathered his things to leave, Whit turned back to her at the door. "Goodnight, Lila. And thanks for dinner. It was perfect."

"Goodnight, Whit," she replied, watching as he walked to his car. She closed the door, leaning against it for a moment, her mind racing with the events of the evening.

From down the hall, she could hear Camille and her friends laughing and talking, oblivious to the moment they had interrupted.

Lila smiled to herself, feeling a sense of hope and excitement for the future. She knew that whatever happened next, she was ready to embrace it with open arms. And as she turned off the lights and headed to bed, her thoughts were filled with the promise of what could be with Whit Calloway.

For the first time in a long time, Lila lay in bed, a soft smile playing on her lips as she drifted off to sleep, dreaming of new beginnings and the unexpected joys of life.

21

L ila adjusted the straps of her backpack, taking a deep breath of the crisp morning air. The trailhead was quiet this early; the only sounds the chirping of birds and the gentle rustling of leaves in the breeze. The Tetons loomed majestically in the background, their snow-capped peaks glowing in the soft light of dawn.

As she hiked, the familiar crunch of gravel under her boots provided a comforting rhythm. The path wound through dense forests of pine and fir, the earthy smell of the forest floor mingling with the fresh, clean scent of mountain air. She loved this place, where the world felt both vast and intimate, and where every step brought her a little closer to the peace she sought.

As she climbed higher, the forest began to thin, and the views opened up. Lila paused for a moment to take in the sight. The valley spread out below her, a patchwork of green and gold, with Phelps Lake glinting in the sunlight. She could see the small town of Thunder Mountain in the far distance, a reminder of the life waiting for her down there, but up here, it felt a world away.

The trail steepened as she neared her favorite lookout point, a rocky outcrop that jutted over the valley. The last stretch was always the hardest, but the reward at the end made it worth every step. Finally, she reached the top, breathing hard but smiling. She set down her backpack and stood at the edge, looking over the breathtaking panorama.

The Tetons stretched before her; their rugged peaks framed by a sky so blue it seemed almost unreal. She could hear the distant roar of a waterfall and the occasional call of an eagle soaring overhead. The air was cooler up here, carrying the faint scent of wildflowers and pine sap.

Lila sat down on a flat rock, hugging her knees to her chest. This was her sanctuary, the place where she escaped when she needed to think, to sort out her tangled thoughts and feelings. She closed her eyes and let the tranquility of nature in its purest form wash over her.

Memories of her husband surfaced, intertwining with her uncertainties about Whit Calloway. The years alone had dragged by, each one feeling interminable, but now, everything seemed to be changing at a dizzying pace.

Up here, those worries seemed smaller, more manageable. She opened her eyes and looked out at the vast landscape, feeling a sense of calm settle over her. Whatever challenges lay ahead, she knew she could face them. She'd learned the importance of endurance, resilience, and the strength to continue moving forward, one step at a time.

Lila closed her eyes, feeling the presence of the mountains around her as if they were silently bearing witness to the conversation she needed to have. She took a deep breath and quietly began to speak. "Aaron, I've missed you terribly. Not a day goes by that I don't think of you. You were my rock, my partner, my everything."

Her voice trembled as she continued. "I'll never forget you. Your laugh, your strength, the way you could make everything better with just a look. You've been my anchor all these years, even in your absence. But...something's happening, something I didn't expect."

She paused, looking heavenward, searching for the right words. "I've met someone, Aaron. His name is Whit Calloway. He's...complicated, frustrating, and everything I didn't know I needed. He challenges me and makes me feel alive in ways I haven't felt since you. And it scares me because I never thought I could feel this way again."

Tears welled up in her eyes as she pressed on. "I'm not asking to forget you or to replace you. But I need to know that it's okay for me to move on. To find happiness again, even if it's different from what we had."

The wind rustled through the trees, carrying her words away into the vast expanse of the valley below. She felt a strange sense of peace as if Aaron was listening, understanding.

"You were, and always will be, my heartbeat," she whispered, a tear sliding down her cheek. "My first love. Thank you for everything, Aaron. For loving me, for our beautiful daughter, for giving me a life I could cherish. I will keep you in my heart, no matter what. Always."

Lila stood up, feeling a little lighter as if a weight had been lifted from her soul. She took one last look at the stunning view, then shouldered her backpack and headed down the trail, ready to face whatever awaited her in the valley.

22

Capri pushed open the heavy wooden door of Bluebird Bookstore, flanked by pots of colorful flowers. The little bell above tinkled softly, announcing her arrival. She stepped inside, taking a moment to breathe in the familiar scent of aged paper and brewing coffee, a comforting blend that always made her think of lazy Saturday afternoons.

The bookstore was a cozy haven, with warm wood tones dominating the interior. Shelves lined every wall, packed tightly with books of all sizes and genres, both new and used. Plants hung from the ceiling in woven baskets, their green tendrils cascading down and adding to the cozy, lived-in feel of the place.

In one corner, a large bay window with small, square panes let in the afternoon sunlight. A plump gray cat, its fur mottled with white patches, lounged lazily on the window seat, watching the world outside with half-closed eyes. Capri smiled at the cat, knowing Miss Agatha Christie was a fixture of the store as much as the books themselves.

The floorboards beneath her feet creaked as Capri

wandered deeper into the store, her eyes scanning the shelves for the spines of Louis L'Amour novels.

She spotted Jason Griffith behind the counter, his head bent over a ledger. Jason was tall and lean, with a mop of curly hair that he constantly brushed back from his forehead. He looked up as she approached, his expression shifting from focused concentration to a friendly smile.

"Hey, Capri," he greeted her, closing the ledger and standing up. "What brings you in today?"

"I'm looking for some Western novels for Dick," Capri replied, returning his smile. "My stepdad's a big fan, and his birthday is coming up."

Jason nodded, stepping out from behind the counter. "Sure thing, we've got a good selection. Follow me."

As they walked, the floorboards continued their symphony of creaks and groans, a charming reminder of the building's age and history. They reached a section filled with Western novels, their covers depicting rugged cowboys and wide-open landscapes.

"How is Dick these days?" Jason asked.

Capri lowered her head slightly. "He's having a tough time. The cancer is progressing. Unfortunately, days when he's in bad pain are increasing."

Jason's expression turned sympathetic. "I'm sorry to hear that. If there's anything me or my mom can do, please reach out."

"Oma brought a pot of chicken soup and some homemade bread by yesterday. No one beats your mom's cooking," she told him.

She couldn't help but reflect on how Charlie Grace had once been entwined with Jason's life. Despite being so unmatched, Charlie Grace had dated Jason for years. That is until Nick Thatcher arrived on the scene, stealing her heart.

Though it had been some time since the breakup, she

hoped Jason's heart had mended and that he had found some semblance of peace.

"Here we are," Jason said, gesturing to the shelf. "Let me know if you need any help finding specific titles."

"Thanks," Capri said, already reaching for a book with a weathered cover.

She plucked four books from the shelf and followed Jason to the check-out counter. "Have you done any birdwatching lately?"

Jason's eyes lit up. "Oh, yes! Just yesterday, I went to the cemetery with Momma and spotted a gray-crowned rosy-finch. Sightings of the delicate pink-and-brown songbird are rare. I was thrilled and captured several shots." As evidence, he pulled out his phone and showed her picture after picture. "See this one? It had a particularly beautiful song." He closed his phone. "Despite their tiny size, these birds are fearless," he told her.

Capri nodded with exaggerated enthusiasm. How in the world had her good friend dated this guy for so long and not gone batty listening to all his bird trivia? That, and the fact he still lived with his mother. There had been no contest when Nick showed up.

She smiled, too kind to let him know her private thoughts.

Their conversation was interrupted by the sound of the door opening, followed by the cheerful jingle of the bell. Capri turned and spotted a striking young woman stepping inside. Her short, stylish haircut—a stunning mix of reddish-brown with blonde highlights—caught the light. Her makeup was immaculate, emphasizing her large, expressive eyes and a confident smile. She wore tight jeans and a form-fitting top that showed off her assets.

As the attractive woman approached the counter, Capri noticed the sway in her step and the confidence in her posture.

"Hey, there," the girl began, her drawl unmistakable. "Could y'all tell me how to get to the veterinary clinic?"

Capri's curiosity piqued. "Oh, do you have a sick animal?" she asked, her voice laced with genuine sympathy.

The young woman shook her head, her smile unwavering. "No, I'm here to see Whit Calloway."

Capri frowned slightly. "How do you know Whit?"

The girl's smile revealed a row of perfect white teeth. "Let me introduce myself. My name is Candy Faye Hutchison. I'm Whit's girlfriend."

Capri's heart skipped a beat. Whit's girlfriend?

She quickly masked her surprise with a polite smile. "Of course," she replied, her mind racing with questions. "The clinic is just a few blocks down the road. Turn left at the end of the street, and you'll see it on your right. It's a big building with a green sign."

"Thank y'all so much," Candy Faye said, her gratitude evident. "I appreciate it."

Capri watched Candy Faye exit the store, her mind buzzing with the new revelation. Whit had a girlfriend? And she was in town? Oh, this could be bad.

She glanced at the clock, knowing that the news would travel fast. By dinnertime, everyone in Thunder Mountain would be talking about the unexpected arrival.

She quickly sent a text to Reva, Charlie Grace, and Lila. "*Urgent—meet me at the Rustic Pine. ASAP! Details to follow.*"

As Capri paid for the books, her thoughts were a whirlwind of concern for her friend. It had taken a lot of prodding to get Lila out of her comfort zone and open to a new life chapter. Based on the look in her friend's eyes every time Whit's name was mentioned, it was apparent Lila had finally turned the page. He was fast becoming more than just her boss.

But now, the dynamics in her budding relationship were about to shift. She hoped Lila would be ready for what was coming. She hated to think of her friend being hurt again.

L ila pushed open the bar door, instantly enveloped by the comforting scent of wood smoke and grilling hamburgers. The dim lighting cast a cozy glow over the room as she scanned the tables for her friends. It didn't take long to spot them, waving her over from their corner table.

"Hey, Lila!" Reva motioned her over from where she sat, flanked by Capri and Charlie Grace.

Lila approached, noting the odd expressions etched on her friends' faces. Capri wouldn't meet her gaze. Instead, she focused on her long-neck bottle.

Trying to mask her concern, Lila slid into the empty chair, placing her purse under the varnished wooden table. "Why the urgency to meet?"

Before they could answer, the bar owner placed a mug of beer in front of her.

"Hey, Annie," Lila said.

Annie stopped her from reaching for her wallet with a hand on her shoulder. "It's on the house," she said with a sympathetic smile.

"Thanks," she said, a bit puzzled.

Annie nodded toward the bar. "If you girls need anything else, just holler." She patted Lila's shoulder before returning to the bar, her black Lab, Bartender, trailing at her feet.

Lila slipped her purse from her shoulder, taking in the familiar surroundings—walls adorned with western-themed paintings and photographs of cowboys and horses. A George Strait song played from the old-fashioned jukebox in the corner.

"Sorry I'm late," she explained. "I got here as fast as I could. I think Camille is coming down with something. I had to make a run to the store for some Pepto."

Reva coughed, clearing her throat. She nervously glanced between the other two.

Lila looked around the table, noting her friends' pained expressions. "Did someone die...or what?"

When no one immediately responded, she nervously added, "Okay, now you're making me scared."

Reva leaned in, her voice loud enough to be heard over the music. "No one died. But, honey, we have something we need to tell you."

Capri nodded. "Yeah, about Whit Calloway."

Lila leaned forward, her heart pounding. "What about Whit?"

Capri's hands tightened on her beer bottle. "His girlfriend showed up in town today."

Lila's breath hitched. "Girlfriend? What do you mean, girlfriend?"

"Her name's Candy Faye Hutchison," Capri said, looking pained. "She's got short, snappy reddish-brown hair with blonde highlights, tight jeans, and let's just say she's got a lot filling her top."

Charlie Grace reached for Lila's hand. "Capri said she walked into the bookstore asking for directions to the clinic, claiming to be Whit's girlfriend."

Lila felt like the floor had dropped out from under her. Her voice grew tight. "But...he never mentioned any girlfriend. Not once."

Reva picked at her napkin. "I looked her up on social media. She's from a well-to-do Texas family. There are lots of pictures of her and Whit together."

Lila's head spun. The bar's warm, comforting atmosphere felt suddenly oppressive.

"Why didn't he tell me?" Lila's voice was barely a whisper. "I've been making baby steps toward. . .something with him. How could he not mention he had a girlfriend?"

Capri reached for Lila's other hand. "We were just as shocked, Lila."

Lila pulled her hands away, a mix of anger and hurt swelling inside her. "How could he do this? Why would he act interested if he had a girlfriend? He almost kissed me! If Camille hadn't walked in—" She put a hand to her stomach. "How am I going to work with him? How will I act like nothing happened between us?" She was aware her voice was getting louder. She didn't care.

Annie glanced over from the bar but didn't approach. Her black Lab, Bartender, laying by her feet, perked up as if he too sensed the unease.

Lila took a deep breath, trying to steady herself. "I knew I shouldn't trust him. The first time I met him at the rodeo, I knew—"

"Maybe there's an explanation, Lila," Reva suggested, leaning close, her voice gentle. "Maybe it's not what it seems."

Lila shook her head. "It doesn't matter. He should've told me. I deserved the truth."

Capri nodded, squeezing her hand. "You're right, Lila. We're here for you."

Lila managed a weak smile, grateful for her friends despite

the turmoil swirling inside her. "Thanks, guys. I just...I need some time to process this."

Annie approached, this time with a tray of nachos. "On the house," she said softly, setting the tray down. "And if you need anything, anything at all, just let me know."

Lila nodded, her eyes welling up. "Thanks, Annie."

As her friends dug into the nachos, Lila sat back, the reality of Whit's betrayal sinking in.

Whit had a girlfriend?

She thought they'd been getting to know each other, and the whole time he'd been hiding a very big secret.

Nothing made sense anymore.

24

T he following morning, Lila Bellamy stepped into the vet clinic, her mind still reeling from learning about Whit's girlfriend.

Whit was already there, leaning over a chart at the reception desk. His tall frame and cowboy demeanor were typically a source of silent attraction, but today she could only feel a sharp pang of annoyance and regret. When he glanced up and offered a warm smile, she felt her temper flare.

"Morning, Lila," he greeted, his Texas drawl as smooth as ever.

"Morning," she replied curtly, avoiding his eyes as she walked past him and headed to the back room.

Lila could feel Whit's confused gaze following her, but she refused to engage. She busied herself with organizing supplies, trying to focus on anything but the anger bubbling inside her.

A few minutes later, Whit's voice came from the doorway. "Lila, is something wrong?"

She didn't look up. "Everything's fine. Just a lot on my mind."

"Doesn't seem like everything's fine," he pressed, his tone

gentle but insistent. "You gave me the cold shoulder when you walked in."

Lila slammed a drawer shut and turned her fiercest glare on him. "I don't want to talk about it," she said, her voice tight.

Whit raised his hands in a placating gesture, concern etched across his face. "All right. But if something's bothering you, you know you can talk to me, right?"

She scoffed, the sound bitter. "Funny. You don't seem to think that applies to you."

He blinked, clearly taken aback. "What do you mean by that?"

Lila turned away, her shoulders tense. That's when she noticed a pink cell phone on the counter. "Nothing. Just forget it."

But Whit wasn't letting it go. "Lila, come on. Just tell me what's going on."

She sighed heavily, her frustration evident. "I said drop it, Whit."

A thick, uncomfortable silence settled between them. Lila could feel Whit's eyes on her, searching for answers she wasn't ready to give. From the corner of her eye, she saw him run a hand through his hair, a gesture she knew meant he was trying to figure out what to do next.

"All right," he said softly, backing off. "But like I said. If you ever want to talk, I'm here."

Lila kept her back to him and didn't respond. She heard him leave the room, and a wave of guilt washed over her. She hated conflict, especially with someone at work, but the thought of Candy Faye whatever-her-name-was claiming to be Whit's girlfriend made her blood boil. How could he not have mentioned the minor fact he was dating someone else?

The day dragged on with a palpable tension hanging in the air. Lila went through the motions of her duties, her interactions with Whit limited to the essentials. Every time he tried to engage her in conversation, she shut him down with curt, one-word answers.

By the end of the day, Lila felt exhausted, the weight of her emotions bearing down on her. She left the clinic without a word, her heart heavy and her mind a whirl of conflicting emotions. She knew she couldn't keep this up for long and hoped with time she could move past it.

But right now, all she could think about was the conjured image of the woman Capri described and that pink phone on the counter.

25

C apri strolled down Main Street, her eyes scanning the storefronts when she spotted a striking woman with a stylish short haircut stepping out of a parked car. It took only a moment for Capri to recognize her.

Candy Faye Hutchison.

Her pulse quickened as she watched Candy Faye stride confidently toward the vet clinic.

"This should be interesting," Capri muttered to herself, deciding to follow and see what drama might unfold.

As she turned for the clinic, she spotted Reva and Charlie Grace emerging from Reva's office across the street. Capri waved them over with an eager smile. "C'mon, she's heading into the vet clinic.

Reva frowned, clearly confused. "Who?"

Capri grabbed Reva's arm. "Whit's girlfriend."

Charlie Grace parked her hands on her hips. "What are you planning to do?"

"Spy," Capri replied with a mischievous glint in her eye.

"But where's Lila?" Reva asked.

"When I talked to her this morning, she said she didn't sleep last night, so she's going in late."

"Understandable," Charlie Grace said. "She's been under a lot of pressure, what with school and now this thing with Whit and a surprise girlfriend."

Capri gave a hearty nod. "So, are you guys with me? I'm heading over to see what's up."

Reva and Charlie Grace exchanged hesitant looks, but curiosity got the better of them. They quickly joined Capri, who led them closer to the clinic. The trio darted behind a large pine tree, watching Candy Faye disappear through the clinic door.

They were about to make their move when they noticed something unusual. Just a few feet away, peering into one of the clinic's windows, were Oma Griffith, Betty Dunning, and Dorothy Vaughn—the notorious Knit Wits of Thunder Mountain.

"What in the world— " Charlie Grace muttered, her eyes wide.

Capri stifled a giggle. "Looks like we're not the only ones interested in this little soap opera."

The trio hurried over to the window. Oma, who was closest to them, jumped and put a hand on her chest. "You girls scared me to death!"

"Shh." Dorothy pointed to the open window. "Be quiet or they'll hear us."

"What are you doing here?" Reva asked.

Betty smirked. "Likely, the same as you three."

"We heard from Nicola that Whit's girlfriend is in town," Oma explained, her voice low and conspiratorial. "We're concerned for Lila and came to check out the situation."

"All right, ladies, let's join forces," Capri said, leaning into the open window. The others followed suit, curiosity burning in their eyes.

Inside, they spotted Candy Faye. "Whit, calm down," she said, her voice sweet but tinged with frustration. "I'm just here to get my phone. I must've left it when I was here."

The women crowded closer and stood on tippy toes, peering inside.

Candy Faye batted her eyes. "But, while I'm here, I think—"

Whit's voice was firm, unwavering. "You shouldn't have come here, Candy. I told you in Texas, what we had was over."

Candy Faye pouted, stepping closer to Whit and using her assets to full effect.

Oma snorted. "What a hussy."

"Shh," Dorothy repeated.

"Come on, Whit," Candy Faye whined. "Can't we talk about this? I love you. We were good together."

The women outside watched with bated breath as Whit took a step back, shaking his head. "No, Candy Faye. This conversation is over. Get your phone and go."

A throat cleared behind them and they all jumped. Without warning, Oma punched the intruder in the chest.

Fleet Southcott, the town cop, looked at her over the top of his sunglasses.

Oma covered her mouth. "Oh, my goodness. I'm so sorry, Fleet. It was an instant reflex."

"Shh!" Dorothy held her finger to her mouth.

Fleet turned his over-the-sunglasses look to Dorothy. "Did you just shush me?"

"Sorry, Fleet. But they're going to hear us," Dorothy warned in a loud whisper.

"What are you ladies doing?" he asked, his tone a mix of curiosity and exasperation.

Capri straightened up, a sly grin spreading across her face. "Just a little community watch, Fleet," she whispered. "Making sure everything is in order."

Fleet raised an eyebrow, clearly unconvinced but not

entirely unsympathetic. "Well, I suggest you stop peering into windows and move along before you have to explain yourselves to the new vet."

As they reluctantly pulled away from the window, Capri couldn't resist a final glance back, hoping Whit continued to stand his ground once they were gone. "I guess we've heard enough," she said, linking arms with Reva and Charlie Grace. "Come on, ladies. We'll stay close by, just in case Miss Candy Faye Hutchison doesn't take no for an answer."

Fleet chuckled, shaking his head as he watched the group disperse. "In this town, I wouldn't expect anything less."

26

Lila woke to the insistent beeping of her alarm clock, the red numbers flashing 8:30 AM. She groaned and rubbed her eyes, feeling the weight of sleepless hours pressing down on her. Camille had already left for school, leaving the house eerily quiet.

Lila sighed and swung her legs over the side of the bed, wincing as her bare feet touched the cold floor. She'd been up all night, her mind a whirl of thoughts and emotions.

Whit Calloway had a girlfriend. The words echoed in her mind, a bitter reminder of how foolish she'd been. She'd only known Whit for a short time, yet she'd let herself get carried away, opening her heart to a man she barely knew. What had she been thinking? She had no business entertaining feelings for someone so soon after meeting.

After tossing and turning, she'd finally given up on sleep and driven to her favorite lookout spot. The place where she felt closest to her late husband, where she could pour out her heart and find a semblance of peace. She had talked to him again, her words carried away by the cool night breeze, her tears blending with the mist that hung over the mountains.

She'd told Aaron everything and admitted what a fool she'd been. Confessing her regret had been cathartic, eliminating some of her self-pity.

She didn't need a man—especially one with a secret girlfriend.

Now, in the harsh light of morning, she felt nothing but determination. She needed to focus on her daughter, on her schooling. Soon, she'd be a certified large animal vet, and that would open up more opportunities.

She'd always thought she'd remain in Thunder Mountain forever, but maybe it was time to consider employment in nearby Jackson. She certainly couldn't remain working for Whit Calloway, not when he'd proven himself untrustworthy.

For years, she had worked for Doc Tillman, enduring his constant belittling. She had thought that taking over the clinic would be her chance to finally prove herself. But now, with Whit in charge, that dream seemed more distant than ever. It was time she put herself first. Enough was enough.

Dragging herself out of bed, Lila dressed quickly, her movements mechanical. She avoided the mirror, not wanting to see the evidence of her sleepless night reflected back at her. By the time she arrived at the clinic, it was already 9:00 AM, an hour later than usual.

The clinic was bustling with activity, the waiting room filled with concerned pet owners and their furry companions. Lila took a deep breath and squared her shoulders, pushing her emotions aside. She had a job to do.

"Morning, Lila," Carla, the new receptionist, greeted her with a bright smile. "Rough night?"

"You could say that," Lila replied, forcing a smile. "What's on the schedule for today?"

"Well, we've got some regular pet checkups this morning and a couple of surgeries later this afternoon. Dr. Calloway wanted to go over some new protocols with you. He's in his office."

Lila nodded, her stomach tightening at the thought of facing Whit. She thanked Carla and headed down the hall, her steps heavy. She didn't have to like working with Lover Boy, she simply had to endure it.

She knocked lightly on Whit's office door.

"Come in," his voice called out.

Lila pushed the door open and stepped inside. Whit looked up from his desk, a mixture of surprise and concern crossing his face. "Lila, you're late. Everything okay?"

"I'm fine," she replied curtly. "Just had a rough night. What did you want to discuss?"

Whit leaned back in his chair, studying her. "I wanted to go over some changes in our procedures, but that can wait. Are you sure you're okay? You look exhausted."

"I said I'm fine," Lila snapped, immediately regretting her tone. She took a deep breath and softened her voice. "Sorry, I didn't mean to be short. I didn't get a lot of sleep last night."

Whit nodded, his expression unreadable. "I understand. If you need some time, we can handle things here. You don't have to push yourself."

"I'm here to work," Lila replied firmly. "Let's get on with it."

Whit hesitated for a moment before nodding. He handed her a stack of papers, letting his fingers linger as their hands met. "These are the new protocols I've been working on. Take a look and let me know what you think. I really want your input before moving forward with these ideas."

Lila took the papers, her hands trembling slightly. She nodded and left his office, retreating to the small break room at the back of the clinic. She sank into a chair and stared at the documents, the words blurring together.

Lila took a deep breath. All she needed was to get through

this day, and then she'd figure out her next steps—with the focus on her daughter, her schooling, and her future. She couldn't afford to let her emotions get in the way.

There was a light rap at the door. "Lila?"

She groaned. Why couldn't Whit just leave her alone?

The door pushed open slightly and he peeked his head inside. "Can we talk?"

Lila looked up, her eyes narrowed. "What is it, Whit?"

He stepped inside, closing the door behind him. "I can see something's bothering you. I'd like to help if I can." His caramel eyes held her captive as he moved closer, lifting her chin with his finger. "You can tell me."

Lila clenched her fists, the papers crumpling slightly in her grip. "Help? Really? Because it seems like all you've done since you got here is make things more complicated."

Whit frowned and stepped back. "Complicated? How?"

She stood, the chair scraping loudly against the floor. "I know about Candy Faye. Your girlfriend." The words dripped from her mouth as sour as they sounded.

Whit's expression shifted as he grasped the situation. "Candy Faye? Lila, she's not my girlfriend."

"Oh, really? Then why did she travel hundreds of miles to see you?" Lila's voice was rising, the frustration of the past sleepless night pouring out of her.

Whit held up his hands. "Lila, listen to me. Candy Faye and I dated briefly, yes, but it's been over for months. She showed up out of nowhere, and I had no idea she was coming. I'm sorry you found out this way."

Lila crossed her arms, full of doubt. "If it was over, why didn't you tell me? You had plenty of time to mention you were fresh out of a relationship. Why keep it a secret?"

Whit ran a hand through his hair, sighing deeply. "I didn't think it was relevant. I didn't want to burden you with my past, especially since I'm trying to move forward. But you're right, I should have been honest. I'm sorry."

Lila shook her head, the tension in her chest not easing. She was no fool. Did he really think he could just spackle over the hurt?

She forced her eyes from his. "I don't know what to think, Whit. I need time to process all of this. I need to focus on my daughter, my schooling. We need to pause whatever this is between us."

A ripple of sadness crossed Whit's face, but he nodded. "I understand, Lila. Take all the time you need."

Suddenly, Lila's stomach lurched. She clamped a hand over her mouth and bolted for the bathroom, barely making it in time before she vomited. She leaned over the toilet, her body shaking, and started to cry.

A moment later, she felt a gentle hand on her back. Whit had followed her, his face filled with concern. He knelt beside her, holding her hair back and rubbing her back soothingly. "Are you okay?"

A fat tear clung to her eyelashes. "Camille was under the weather. I—I must've caught whatever my daughter had."

She continued to cry, not caring how she looked. Not caring that Whit was watching.

"Lila, I'm so sorry," he whispered. Her breath caught in her throat as his hand tenderly brushed the side of her face. "I never wanted to hurt you."

Her sobs grew louder as the weight of the past few days crashed down on her. She felt Whit's arms wrap around her, his presence steady and comforting despite everything.

For the first time in a long time, she allowed herself to lean on someone else, even if just for a moment. Lila's thoughts swirled with confusion. Sure, her life was safe—but it was also tepid.

She had spent so long building walls around her heart, convinced that she had to face the world alone, vowing to exhibit strength and independence, but in reality, it had only left her feeling isolated and vulnerable.

Now, with Whit holding her, she rewound her thoughts, realizing how exhausted she was from carrying her burdens alone. She thought about all the times she had stood at her favorite lookout spot, talking to her deceased husband, seeking solace in the memories of their love. She had believed that was the only place she could find peace.

It was terrifying to think about opening herself up again, to trust someone new, especially someone who had already caused her pain. But as she felt Whit's steady presence beside her, she couldn't deny that there was something genuine in his concern. His explanation about Candy Faye might not erase the doubts entirely, but his actions in this moment spoke louder than his words.

He could have left her alone, could have walked when she pushed him away, but he didn't. He stayed, offering her comfort and understanding without expecting anything in return. It was a small gesture, but it felt monumental to Lila.

She took a deep breath, her sobs gradually subsiding into quiet sniffles. The future was still uncertain, and there were many questions left unanswered. Yet, she was beginning to understand how quick she'd been to push Whit away at the first sign of trouble.

She wasn't ready to completely forgive and forget, but maybe, just maybe, she could begin to see a different path forward—one where she didn't have to be alone.

In that small bathroom, with Whit by her side, Lila felt a flicker of hope. It wasn't a promise of a perfect future, but it was a start.

As she leaned against Whit, feeling the steady rhythm of his breathing, she made a silent promise to herself. She would take the time she needed to heal, to think, and to decide what she truly wanted.

No matter what, she wouldn't settle for anything less than what she deserved.

27

I n the days that followed, Lila and Whit found themselves navigating the delicate dance of rebuilding their relationship. The initial awkwardness following the incident with Candy Faye began to dissipate as they spent more time together at the clinic. Whit made a concerted effort to be transparent, sharing details of his life and work that he had previously kept to himself. He often found excuses to join Lila on farm calls, their conversations becoming more relaxed and genuine with each passing day.

One afternoon, as they drove to a remote ranch to tend to a colicky mare, Whit opened up about his time in Texas, explaining his past relationship with Candy Faye. "It wasn't a serious thing," he said, his eyes fixed on the winding mountain road ahead. "She was more interested in the idea of what we could be, rather than what we actually were."

Lila listened quietly, her hands resting in her lap. She appreciated his honesty, even though a part of her still felt a pang of jealousy. "I understand," she replied softly. "I guess I just needed to hear it from you."

Whit reached over, gently squeezing her hand. "Thank you for giving me another chance," he said, his voice sincere.

They drove in comfortable silence for several minutes before Whit glanced over at Lila. "Hey, what do you say you let me take you out for dinner in Jackson on Friday night."

Lila's face brightened, but then she sighed. "Oh, Whit, I'm sorry. I've already committed to going to a book signing with the girls. It's for Roxie Steele, the romance author I told you about. She's just finished her latest novel, and her publisher is offering early copies at the signing in town. The event is being hosted by Bluebird Books, our little bookstore."

Whit smiled. "Sounds fun."

Lila couldn't help but laugh softly. "Sounds...interesting."

Whit, looking incredibly handsome in a snug white T-shirt that accentuated his chest, raised an eyebrow. "What do you mean, interesting?"

"Well," Lila said with a smirk, "I'm not sure anyone will show up. Roxie Steele writes...shall we say, rather saucy material."

"Ah," Whit replied, understanding dawning.

On Friday, the day of the book signing, the new town community center was surprisingly crowded. Lila and her friends arrived, expecting a modest turnout, only to be greeted by a line that snaked around the block.

Inside, the atmosphere buzzed with excitement. Tables were set up with stacks of Roxie Steele's latest novel, *Desire in the Dust*, and a banner reading, "Welcome, Roxie Steele!" hung from the ceiling.

The owner of Bluebird Books, Jason Griffith, wore a delighted look as he manned a makeshift table set up with a cash register.

As Lila, Capri, Reva, and Charlie Grace made their way through the crowd, Lila spotted familiar faces. There was Mrs. Jenkins, the town librarian, clutching a copy of the book with a look of guilty pleasure. Old Mr. Thompson, the retired history teacher, stood in line with a bemused expression, likely wondering how he ended up at a romance book signing.

In the corner, the Knit Wits were gathered, their needles clicking furiously as they sat on folding chairs, chatting, and laughing. Dorothy, the unofficial leader of the group, waved them over. "Girls! You won't believe how spicy this book is. I had to fan myself just reading the first chapter."

Lila chuckled, shaking her head. "Dorothy, I never would have pegged you for a fan of... let's call it, steamy literature."

Dorothy winked. "Honey, life needs a little spice, don't you think? Keeps things interesting."

Reva leaned in, whispering, "Did you see Mildred? She's here, too. I never thought I'd see the day."

Sure enough, Mildred, the town's most conservative resident, stood in line, her face a mix of curiosity and scandalized intrigue. "Oh, my goodness," Lila whispered back. "This is too good."

Capri elbowed her and laughed. "Looks like the lady has fans of the male persuasion as well."

Fleet Southcott and Albie Barton stood in line clutching their copies. Earl Dunlop was right behind them with his book open and reading.

Just as Lila was about to join in the laughter, she felt an elbow in her side. Reva leaned in, her eyes wide with alarm, and pointed across the room. "Lila, look over there. It's her."

Lila followed her friend's gaze and froze. Standing near the entrance, looking entirely too confident for Lila's liking, was a young woman who had to be Candy Faye Hutchison. The girlfriend was back in town, and she was dressed to impress.

She wore a fitted gray tank top that showcased her toned arms and highlighted her elegant collarbone. Paired with this was a stylish denim skirt that hugged her curves just right, ending just above her knees to show off her long legs.

Completing her look, she wore a pair of polished, and obviously expensive, brown cowboy boots that added a touch of Texas flair to her ensemble.

Her reddish-brown hair with blonde highlights was styled in a short, trendy cut that framed her face perfectly. Her makeup was flawless, with a subtle smoky eye that made her hazel eyes pop, and a soft, rosy blush accentuating her high cheekbones. A pair of small, elegant earrings added a touch of sophistication to her look. She exuded confidence and poise, her expression making it clear she was here for a purpose.

Lila's heart sank. "What is she doing back?" she muttered under her breath.

Reva frowned, her eyes narrowing. "She must be here for Whit. I can't think of any other reason she'd come back."

Just then, Candy Faye caught sight of them and sauntered over, a smug smile on her face. "Well, well, if it isn't the famous Lila Bellamy." She held out a hand to shake. "I don't believe we've met."

Lila forced a tight smile, trying to keep her composure. "Candy Faye." She shook, then dropped her hand as quickly as possible. "What brings you back to Thunder Mountain?"

"Oh, you know," Candy Faye drawled, her Texas accent as thick as ever. "Just passing through, thought I'd stop by and see how an old friend was doing."

The implication was clear.

Lila's eyes flashed with annoyance. "I wasn't aware you had any friends in Thunder Mountain."

Her implication was equally clear.

Candy Faye laughed, a tinkling sound that grated on Lila's nerves. "Oh, Lila, always so serious. Lighten up, will you? I was just hoping to catch up with Whit. You know, old times and all."

Capri stepped forward, her hands on her hips. "Well, he's not here, so I guess you'll have to find someone else to bother."

Candy Faye's smile didn't falter. "Oh, that's okay. I know where he lives."

Lila felt a surge of protectiveness and anger. "Candy Faye, Whit and I are—" She paused, realizing she didn't want to reveal too much. "Whit is busy."

"Is he now?" Candy Faye replied, feigning surprise. "Well, I guess I'll just have to wait around and see him when he's not so...busy."

Lila clenched her fists, trying to keep her cool. "I'll text and alert Whit you want to see him."

Candy Faye leaned in closer, her smile turning icy. "Oh, Lila, no need. I know where he lives."

With that, she turned and walked away, leaving Lila seething. Reva placed a reassuring hand on her shoulder. "Don't let her get to you, Lila."

Charlie Grace patted her on the back. "The nerve of that woman. Whit dumped her and she keeps coming back for more? Don't let her bother you, Lila. You have nothing to worry about."

"Yeah," Capri said. "He'll send her packing, just like last time."

Lila took a deep breath, willing herself to calm down. "I know. But I can't help but feel like she's ready to stir up trouble."

Reva nodded. "We'll keep an eye on her. But tonight, let's focus on having a good time. Candy Faye isn't worth ruining our evening over."

Lila managed a small smile. "You're right."

Still, Lila couldn't shake the feeling of unease. Candy Faye's return was trouble. She'd come all the way from Texas, her mind set on one thing...reclaiming Whit Calloway. It didn't matter that their tumultuous relationship ended or that Whit had started a new life here in this small mountain town. Candy

Faye had decided that Whit belonged to her, and she wasn't about to let him slip through her fingers.

Before she could voice her concerns, Lila felt a tap on her shoulder. Turning, she found herself face-to-face with Roxie Steele herself, a petite woman with a shock of red hair and a mischievous smile. "You must be Lila Bellamy," she said, extending a hand. "Whit told me all about you."

Lila tried to hide her surprise as she shook Roxie's hand. "You know Whit?"

Roxie grinned. "Oh yes, I met him in the Rusty Pine a few nights ago. He's quite taken with you."

The woman nodded subtly towards the door. "But it looks like that woman has an agenda."

With a conspiratorial glint in her eye, Roxie leaned closer and pressed a book into Lila's hands. "Darlin', it's time to fight fire with fire. Read Chapter 23. It'll tell you everything you need to know."

28

The next morning, Lila woke up with that sense of unease that she couldn't quite shake. The community picnic was today, and while it was one of her favorite events of the year, she couldn't help but feel a storm was brewing—especially given Candy Faye was back in town.

Despite Whit's reassurances on the phone that he intended to send his former girlfriend away—this time a little more forcefully—Lila had seen the determined look in her nemesis' eyes.

That woman wasn't going away easily.

Lila lay in bed for a moment longer, listening to the birds chirping outside her window, before finally getting up and stretching. The autumn sun filtered through the curtains, casting a golden glow across her bedroom that promised a good day ahead.

She took a deep breath, trying to steady her nerves. Yes, today was supposed to be fun—a day filled with laughter, games, and good food—but the nagging feeling in her gut told her otherwise.

As she got dressed, her thoughts drifted back to Whit and

the deep talks they'd had since their misunderstanding. She'd
felt so sure about the relationship they were building. But the
arrival of Candy Faye Hutchison, with her perfect hair and
relentless determination, had thrown a wrench into things.

Lila brushed her hair with quick, resolute strokes, hoping
Whit had already sent Candy Faye packing a second time. If
not, she wouldn't let Whit's former girlfriend ruin this day or
her relationship with Whit. She chose a light pink sundress
with a matching sweater, hoping to embrace the festive spirit of
the picnic despite her lingering anxiety.

She was about to head downstairs when she noticed Roxie
Steele's novel on the bedside table. Curious, she picked it up
and turned to the chapter Roxie had recommended. A few
paragraphs in and she was blushing.

Still, she couldn't seem to put the book down. She read for
several more minutes until a slow smile formed.

Well, Roxie Steele...you're smarter than you let on.

Lila set the book aside and quickly returned to her closet.
Why was she standing around feeling helpless? Sure, this idea
was way out of her comfort zone, but she'd lived a passive life
letting others dictate her happiness far too long. She could
depend on Whit to end the situation...or she could fight fire by
starting a little blaze of her own.

It was time to take action.

She dug in the back until she found a dress she hadn't worn
in years, if ever. It was one she'd ordered on a whim on a day
when she'd felt frumpy and wanted to impress Aaron. When
the package came and she'd tried the garment on, she quickly
realized the outfit was outside her comfort zone.

But now, the form-fitting dress might be just the thing,
especially with the low-cut bodice.

After ripping off the sundress and tossing it on her bed, she
pulled the tight fabric up and struggled with the zipper. After

successfully closing the back, she took a look at herself in the floor-length mirror attached to her bedroom door.

She frowned.

Clearly, the dress was styled for someone far more endowed. Someone like Candy Faye, she thought as she scrambled to her dresser. She pulled out the top drawer and rifled through her intimate garments until her hand landed on a particular piece of lingerie.

Lila grinned and headed for the bathroom where she exchanged her current bra for the new one. Still smiling, she unrolled a wad of toilet paper and filled the gap in the left cup, then the right.

With her hands, she pushed up both cups and glanced in the mirror. Satisfied, she zipped up her dress again, spritzed herself heavily with perfume, and headed downstairs.

Thanks to Roxie Steele and her novel, she now realized two could play this game.

Whit arrived right on time, pulling up in his blue pickup. Lila felt her heart lighten at the sight of him. He climbed out, his familiar grin spreading across his face as he walked towards her.

"Morning, beautiful," he said, leaning in to kiss her cheek. He leaned back and whistled. "Wow!"

"Morning," Lila replied, smiling up at him. "Ready for the picnic?"

Whit chuckled. "Always. You know I can't resist Mrs. Jenkins' famous peach cobbler."

Whit glanced around. "Where's Camille?"

"She rode to the picnic with friends. We'll meet her there."

They climbed into the truck, and Lila felt a small weight lift off her shoulders. She looked like a million bucks, and Whit had appreciated her effort.

As they drove towards the park, she held Whit's hand, feeling the warmth and strength in his grip. She glanced over at him, appreciating his easy smile and the way his eyes crinkled at the corners when he laughed. The scenic route to the park was lined with sunflowers, and Lila tried to let the beauty distract her from her worries.

The park was already bustling with activity when they arrived. Families were setting up picnic blankets, children were running around playing games, and the mouthwatering scent of grilled burgers and hot dogs filled the air.

Lila spotted Charlie Grace wheeling her dad, Clancy Rivers, towards a group of men chatting animatedly near the barbecue pit. She exchanged waves with them.

As she and Whit strolled hand in hand through the park, Lila felt a sense of contentment, despite being on the lookout for Candy Faye. According to Whit, his former girlfriend had yet to show up at his place. When she did, he promised to deal with the situation pronto.

"There won't be any doubt where I stand," he told her. "I'll put an end to this...once and for all."

She believed him and everything seemed perfect. That was until she heard the unmistakable click of boots on the pavement behind her. She turned to see Candy Faye Hutchison, her glamorous rival from Texas, making a beeline for them.

"Whit, honey, I didn't expect to see you here. Remember when we used to go to picnics back in Texas together?" Candy Faye's voice dripped with honeyed nostalgia as she ignored Lila's presence entirely.

Lila's grip on Whit's hand tightened, her knuckles turning white. She forced a smile, though her insides flashed with irritation.

Whit's jaw tightened. "That was a long time ago, Candy Faye. Things have changed."

"Have they? Some things never change," Candy Faye said with a smirk, her gaze locked on Lila.

The tension between the two women was palpable. Whit glanced nervously between them, sensing the brewing storm.

Candy Faye looked her up and down. "Love the outfit. Of course, the fit is a bit off, don't you think." She let her gaze drop to Lila's bustline.

Whit stepped forward. "Look, the thing between us is over, Candy. You need to go home."

Lila couldn't help it. Her ire was up, and suddenly her mouth had a mind of its own. She would no longer be a door-mat. "Candy Faye, why are you really here? Because it sure isn't for the potato salad," Lila said, her voice steady despite the anger bubbling inside her.

"Oh, I just came to see if Whit remembers what it's like to be with a real woman," Candy Faye replied, her tone dripping with challenge.

Before Whit could hold her back, Lila stepped closer, her smile vanishing. "Oh, trust me, he knows. Why don't you take your memories back to the land of steers and beers, and leave us alone?"

"Make me," Candy Faye shot back, her eyes glinting with defiance.

"What are you? A child?"

Candy Faye nearly hissed like the snake she was. "No, dear. I'm all woman."

"A woman who lost her man," Lila snarled.

A small crowd had gathered, sensing the impending confrontation. The argument grew louder, the tension thicker.

"Lila, Candy Faye, let's not do this here." Whit tried to inter-vene, his voice pleading.

But it was too late. Candy Faye shoved Lila, who stumbled back but quickly regained her footing. Lila's eyes narrowed as she spotted the mud pit nearby, set up for the tug-of-war competition.

"You want to play dirty? Fine, let's play dirty," Lila said, her voice low and dangerous. She'd stood aside and taken whatever was dished her way long enough. It was time to stand up for herself.

Without warning, Lila lunged at Candy Faye, tackling her into the mud pit. The crowd gasped, then erupted into laughter and cheers.

Reva raced over. "Lila! What are you doing?"

Capri joined them. "You go, girl!"

Camille rushed forward, grinning with excitement. "Yeah, go Mom! You can take her."

"Well, this is more entertaining than the three-legged race," Albie Barton said to Whit, chuckling. "I might have to make this the headline story in next week's paper."

Whit watched in disbelief as Lila and Candy Faye wrestled in the mud. He tried to pull Lila away but was unsuccessful. "Stay back," she warned, her voice firm and resolute, determined to see this through.

The scene was chaotic, messy, and hilarious. Mud flew everywhere as the two women grappled, each trying to gain the upper hand.

"You're crazy, Lila!" Candy Faye gasped, struggling to free herself.

"Maybe, but I'm not losing Whit to you!" Lila let out a laugh, her determination unwavering.

The crowd, now fully invested, cheered and jeered as Lila and Candy Faye continued their muddy brawl. Both women were covered head to toe in mud, slipping and sliding as they fought.

Eventually, a few brave souls from the crowd helped pull the muddy combatants apart. Both women were exhausted, panting heavily and covered in mud, but Lila stood tall, victorious. She wiped her hands off, completely satisfied with the results of her impulsive actions.

"You didn't have to do that, you know," Whit said, grinning as he helped Lila up.

"Oh, but it was worth it," Lila replied, breathless but smiling. "I'm tired of stepping around roadblocks. It was past time to run some down."

"This isn't over, Lila," Candy Faye muttered, wiping mud from her face.

"Yes, it is. Now, go clean yourself up," Lila said firmly, her eyes locked on Candy Faye's. "And then go back to where you came from. Because if you don't...I'll make sure that mean mouth of yours is filled with worse than mud." She offered up a fist as proof.

The crowd applauded as Candy Faye slunk away, humiliated.

"Well, I guess my woman took care of things," Whit said, laughing.

Whit pulled Lila next to him and they shared a muddy but heartfelt kiss, solidifying their bond in front of everyone. Only then did Lila see a trail of dirt-caked toilet paper trailing from the top of her dress. She tucked it back in place, laughing.

As they walked away from the mud pit, Capri patted Lila on the back. "Remind me never to cross you, Lila Bellamy."

"Yeah, I can't believe you did that," Charlie Grace exclaimed.

"You were awesome, Mom," Camille said. "You really stood up for yourself."

Lila laughed with exhilaration. "Just another day in Thunder Mountain."

Whit intertwined his arm with hers. "C'mon, Mud Warrior. Let's get you home and changed."

As the festivities resumed around her, Lila felt an overwhelming sense of triumph. She knew there wouldn't be any more trouble from Candy Faye. She'd made sure of that.

Despite being muddy and disheveled, Lila had defended her love and shown everyone, including herself, that she was willing to fight for what mattered most.

29

Eight months later

Lila stood at the edge of the stage, her heart pounding in her chest as she scanned the sea of faces sitting in the audience at Folsom Field Stadium. The sun shone brightly, casting a warm glow over the University of Colorado's commencement ceremony. She took a deep breath, reminding herself to savor this moment. It was the culmination of years of hard work, sacrifice, and unwavering determination.

As her name was called, the front row erupted into applause. Lila stepped forward, her graduation gown billowing around her. She glanced toward all her friends and family, their faces beaming with pride. Whit was there, his eyes shining with love. Next to him were Charlie Grace, Reva, Capri, and her beloved daughter Camille, who was cheering the loudest of all. Her heart skipped a beat when she saw Doc Tillman and his wife, Winnie, sitting beside them, their presence a touching surprise.

With each step she took toward the podium, memories of her journey flashed through her mind—the long nights studying, the moments of doubt, and the relentless pursuit of her dream. As she accepted her degree in large animal veterinary studies, she felt a surge of triumph. But the moment wasn't just about her achievement...it was about everyone who had supported her along the way.

Dr. DiStefano smiled warmly as he handed her the Chancellor's Academic Recognition Award, acknowledging her 4.0 GPA. "Ladies and gentlemen," he announced. "Please welcome Lila Bellamy, this year's recipient of the Chancellor's Academic Recognition Award, to give her speech."

The crowd cheered.

Lila stepped up to the podium, adjusting the microphone. She took another deep breath, feeling the weight of the moment. The stadium quieted, and she began.

"Thank you, Chancellor, faculty, family, and friends," she started, her voice steady. "Today is a day of celebration, not just for me, but for all of us who have walked this journey together. It's a day to acknowledge the challenges we've overcome and the dreams we've realized."

She paused, looking out at the audience. "When I started this journey, I was a single mother, widowed, and trying to find my way. There were moments when I doubted if I could make it, but I learned that perseverance and passion can carry you through the darkest times."

Lila's eyes found Whit's, and she smiled. "I also learned the importance of community. To my dear friends Charlie Grace, Reva, and Capri, you have been my rocks, my confidants, and my cheerleaders. To my daughter Camille, you are my inspiration. And to Whit, thank you for believing in me."

She took a deep breath. Her gaze met her daughter's before drifting back to Whit. "To quote Dory in *Finding Nemo*, 'When I look at you, I can feel it. I look at you, and I'm home.'"

She glanced at Doc Tillman, her voice filled with gratitude.

"Doc Tillman, your mentorship and support have been invaluable. I wouldn't be here without your guidance."

Lila's gaze swept across the crowd, taking in the sea of graduates. "To my fellow graduates, remember that success is not just about the destination but the journey. It's about the people who walk alongside you, the lessons you learn, and the impact you make."

She took a deep breath, her heart full. "As we step into the future, let's carry forward the spirit of determination, compassion, and resilience. Let's make a difference in the world, one step at a time."

She paused and cleared her throat. "And never forget your worth. Remember to stand up for yourselves."

The crowd erupted into applause, and Lila stepped back from the podium, feeling a sense of accomplishment and fulfillment she had never known before. As the ceremony continued, she returned to her seat, her heart light and her spirit soaring.

After the ceremony, Lila found herself surrounded by her loved ones. Whit pulled her into a tight embrace. "You were amazing, Lila. I'm so proud of you."

Charlie Grace, Reva, and Capri joined in, their laughter and hugs filling her with warmth. Camille hugged her tightly. "Mom, you did it!"

Doc Tillman approached, his eyes twinkling with pride. "You've come a long way, Lila. I always knew you had it in you."

Lila smiled, tears of joy streaming down her face. "Thank you, Doc. Thank you all. I couldn't have done this without you."

As the crowd began to disperse, Whit took Lila's hand, pulling her gently aside. "Lila," he said, his voice filled with emotion. "I've been thinking a lot about everything you've accomplished and what you've meant to the clinic and to Thunder Mountain. It's time for a change." He paused, taking a deep breath. "I want you to know that from this moment on, you're not just an employee. I'm making you a full partner in the veterinary clinic. You've earned it, Lila, and I can't think of anyone better to share this with."

Lila's eyes widened in disbelief as Whit's words sank in. "A full partner?" she echoed, her voice trembling with emotion. "Whit, I don't know what to say. This is... it's everything I've ever dreamed of." Tears of gratitude welled up in her eyes. "Thank you. Thank you for believing in me, for giving me this opportunity. I promise I'll give it my all. We're going to make the clinic better than ever."

She reached up and hugged him tightly, feeling a mix of joy, relief, and overwhelming gratitude. "I won't let you down," she whispered, her voice filled with determination.

As they stood together, the sun now high over the stadium, Lila knew that this glorious day was just the beginning of a new chapter. With her degree in hand and the support of those she loved, she was ready to face whatever the bright future held.

She had fought for her dreams and won.

READY FOR MORE OF the *TETON MOUNTAIN SERIES*? Check out book four: *AS THE SUN RISES* and read about Capri's surprise adventures.

AUTHOR'S NOTE

Hello, Readers!

A heartfelt thank you for reading the Teton Mountain Series. These books celebrate the invaluable role of friendships. I am thankful to have girlfriends I've known since high school. These women bless me beyond what I can describe.

The spark for these stories was my own experiences of profound friendship, a theme I've always wanted to explore in my writing.

A trip to Yellowstone National Park and the Teton Mountain National Park in Wyoming inspired the setting. For any of you who have followed me, you know I thrill to take my readers to places I love to vacation. In these books, you'll be whisked away to the majestic Teton Mountains, you'll dine in the trendy restaurants in Jackson Hole, and see bears and moose in secluded pinewood forests. You'll experience herds of buffalo roaming the meadows of Hayden Valley and hike the backcountry trails around crystal blue lakes lined with pastel-colored lupine blooms. The town of Thunder Mountain is a fictionalized community based upon DuBois, Wyoming—a charming western town with wooden boardwalks and quaint buildings lining its Main Street. I took a little liberty as an author and relocated it to where Moran is now on the map.

Mostly, I created four women friends who have become so very dear to me as I've placed them on the pages of these books —Charlie Grace, Reva, Lila and Capri.

I hope you enjoy the time spent with us!

Kellie Coates Gilbert

ALSO BY KELLIE COATES GILBERT

Dear Readers,

Thank you for reading this story. If you'd like to read more of my books, please check out these series.

To purchase at special discounts: www.kelliecoatesgilbertbooks.com

TETON MOUNTAIN SERIES

Where We Belong – Book 1

Echoes of the Heart – Book 2

Holding the Dream – Book 3

As the Sun Rises – Book 4

MAUI ISLAND SERIES

Under the Maui Sky – Book 1

Silver Island Moon – Book 2

Tides of Paradise – Book 3

The Last Aloha – Book 4

Ohana Sunrise – Book 5

Sweet Plumeria Dawn – Book 6

Songs of the Rainbow – Book 7

Hibiscus Christmas – Book 8

PACIFIC BAY SERIES

Chances Are – Book 1

Remember Us – Book 2

Chasing Wind – Book 3

Between Rains – Book 4

SUN VALLEY SERIES

Sisters – Book 1

Heartbeats – Book 2

Changes – Book 3

Promises – Book 4

TEXAS GOLD COLLECTION

A Woman of Fortune – Book 1

Where Rivers Part – Book 2

A Reason to Stay – Book 3

What Matters Most – Book 4

STAND ALONE NOVELS:

Mother of Pearl

AVAILABLE AT ALL MAJOR RETAILERS

FOR EXCLUSIVE DISCOUNTS:

www.kelliecoatesgilbertbooks.com

ABOUT THE AUTHOR

USA Today Bestselling Author Kellie Coates Gilbert has won readers' hearts with her heartwarming and highly emotional stories about women and the relationships that define their lives. As a former legal investigator, Kellie brings a unique blend of insight and authenticity to her stories, ensuring that readers are hooked from the very first page.

In addition to garnering hundreds of five-star reviews, Kellie has been described by RT Book Reviews as a "deft, crisp storyteller." Her books were featured as Barnes & Noble Top Shelf Picks and earned a coveted place on Library Journal's Best Book List.

Born and raised amidst the breathtaking beauty of Sun Valley, Idaho, Kellie draws inspiration from the vibrant landscapes of her youth, infusing her stories with a vivid sense of place. Kellie now lives with her husband of over thirty-five years in Dallas, where she spends most days by her pool drinking sweet tea and writing the stories of her heart.

Learn more about Kellie and her books at www.kelliecoatesgilbert.com

Enjoy special discounts by buying direct from Kellie at www.kelliecoatesgilbertbooks.com

Sign up for her newsletter and be the first to hear about new releases, sales, news, and VIP-only specials. Click here to sign up: VIP READER NEWS

WHERE TO FIND ME:

Kellie Coates Gilbert's Shop
(Enjoy special discounts!)

Kellie's Website

She's Reading with Kellie Coates Gilbert
(Facebook group featuring live author chats)

GILBERT GIRLS- Kellie's reader group on Facebook

Made in the USA
Monee, IL
29 January 2025

11224676R10111